Chimera and Curses

Book 2 of The Ember Files

Shari Marshall

Writing Sparkle Books
sharimarshall.ca
Alberta, Canada

This book contains an excerpt from the forthcoming book in *The Ember Files* by Shari Marshall. The excerpt has been set for this edition only and may not reflect the final content of the forthcoming edition(s).

Marshall, Shari
Chimera and Curses: Book 2 of The Ember Files

eBook ISBN 978-1-7782531-1-9
Paperback ISBN 978-1-7782531-0-2

Fiction | Fantasy | Urban
Fiction | Fantasy | Humour
Fiction | Fantasy | Dragons & Mythical Creatures

Praise for
Chimera and Curses

"The fun of *Chimera and Curses* lies in the details of its characters' lives, and Marshall renders those details with a deft, polished eye for colorful, vivid imagery, especially when it's to get a laugh . . . Readers in search of a witty, laid-back fantasy diversion will find much to love in Shari Marshall's *Chimera and Curses*, a charming comic adventure full of rollicking hijinks" – *IR*, starred review

"Marshall's prose is descriptive and sometimes appealingly jocular . . ." – *Kirkus Reviews*

"Boasting a casual clash of real-world and magical elements, this playful second installment is highly original, with a stellar blend of fantasy action, teasing wisecracks, and romantic tension." – *SPR*, starred review

Dedication

I'm indebted to the following people for their support:

To my husband, Greg, thanks for tolerating my obsession to write this to the end.

To my boys, Ayden and Owen, for always loving my story ideas.

Chimera and Curses

Chapter 1

Everything about this day is unexpected, which isn't remarkable. My life's motto is when crazy calls, Kori answers, and over the last year, I have come to understand this is my normal. I'm Kori Ember, the woman drawn to answer the crazed. Nevertheless, my life is improving. With that acceptance, I typically dress my five-foot-three fit body in studio pants and a tank top to allow for ease of movement in any situation. I prefer barefoot in all seasons, but sandals are tolerable.

I let the seven chakra stones floating over my hand on the air currents drop into my palm appreciating their coolness. This exercise won't be enough for the constant arguing. The last seven months of renovations have been a nightmare, the only thing they've agreed on is purchasing Just Flavours. How Fin and Belamey expect to run this café together is beyond me. *Belamey Adelgrief.* My heart flutters, and I respond with a wave of irritation. Fin insists that I should be reckless and just jump Belamey's bones, but I'm . . . I don't know what I am.

I glance at my best friend, Finley Salinger, known to most people as Fin. Her electric green eyes lock on Belamey's brown ones. She stretches her five-foot-seven frame so she is nose to nose with Belamey, who stands at six foot two. They're talking over each other so loudly that nobody has any idea what's being said. It's just one blur of noise that's headache-inducing. I can't listen to it anymore. I stand and stomp my foot. Because I've been successful in stopping Fin and Belamey's arguing, I ignore the fact that the thin sole on my sandal has absorbed none of the jarring impact from my action. Fin's layered black hair sways wildly as her head snaps in my direction. Belamey gives a more controlled switch, but he focuses on me, nonetheless.

"Just Flavour or Just Flavour-s." I draw out the sound of the s. "Who cares! Move on to revising your menu." Rolling my eyes at them, I huff. "One would think the limited menu options would be more important for the Grand Re-opening." I don't wait for either of them to respond. Moving sides of the table, I sit, but this time my back is to them.

I draw a deep breath, enjoying the smell of coffee clinging to the air. I watch the swirling snowflakes as I make a concentrated effort to disregard Fin and Belamey while they take turns imitating my foot stomp and mini speech. The pair of them teaming up to tease me isn't new. I switch my thoughts to Fin's infatuation with Belamey and how it's changed to a little sister and big brother relationship. I'm trying to sort through her change in attitude, not to mention my involvement with them.

Fin's insistence that Belamey has feelings for me sticks in my mind, as does my indecision. Luckily, I haven't had to give it much thought because Belamey seems aloof lately. Regardless, the three of us, via The Recruiter's assigned team-building exercises, have become a good alliance. We're adept at reading each other's cues. In addition, I'm learning about my magical strengths. Willing to gamble on my abilities, The Recruiter offered me a job on the team he's rebuilding to work from the shadows to keep our people safe. A job I accepted, and with the last year's small missions, I've grown as a Spellbinder.

Before I get lost in my thoughts, the café door bangs open, and a violent gale rips through the room bringing a frosty clean smell with it. Fin crosses the space, locking the door shut and cutting off the storm. I exchange a look with Belamey, letting him know we're no longer alone. I discern someone or something else has entered the café on the wind. My ability to sense life forms is a power I've retained from using the Ember stone last year. Initially, I thought it was people I could sense, but as I've become more familiar with the power, I've realized I can perceive all living matter the world over. However, the strength of this talent has faded. Now, I can only sense loved ones outside of my immediate vicinity, but I can detect any living matter close by.

This current presence is unique. Although I sense it's in the room, I can't detect who or what it is. It isn't revealing itself to us in physical form. Fin, adept at reading her environment, has placed her rump against the wall and armed herself with the throwing knives she keeps hidden on her person. Belamey and I both have magic sparked on our fingers, ready to release orbs at the first sign of trouble. The silence deepens as we survey the space and wait for the unforeseen.

"Reveal yourself." I speak out loud, noting I don't feel foolish, while also noting there was a time when this action would've caused me to question my sanity.

In response to my command, a high-pitched hiccup breaks the silence.

"Lord Bradig?" Belamey directs his words to the air in the room. A knee-high form blinks into sight and out again so quickly that all I glimpse is a flash of blue-grey skin and long, thin, pointy ears.

Hic is the only sound the invisible creature makes.

Belamey has released the magic from his hands, and he has crouched low with an enormous smile painted on his normally sombre face. "Lord Bradig," he whispers, like he's encouraging a scared puppy. "Lord Bradig, it's okay. You're safe here with myself and my friends, Fin Salinger and Kori Ember."

We wait. Fin has taken her cue from Belamey, and her knives have disappeared, along with her defensive stance. I roll my eyes skyward and allow my orbs to dissipate. When my eyes refocus, I see a flat-chested creature with a protruding round belly. Belamey bows to it. I cast my wide-eyed stare at Fin. She smiles and mouths an unknown word at me. The little creature, Lord Bradig, gives an upward flick of his oversized three-fingered, one-thumbed hand, indicating Belamey can stand. Lord Bradig turns toward Fin.

Fin lowers herself to one knee and bends forward at her waist, casting her eyes to the ground. "It's an honour, Lord Bradig."

My eyes are so wide they're aching, and I'm thankful Lord Bradig doesn't turn to me. I work to control my face while he gives an excited stream of hiccups before he coughs and farts.

Lord Bradig turns to Belamey. "I like this one. She is respectful and smart. What might I call her?"

Belamey dips his head toward Fin. "Her name is Finley Salinger."

Lord Bradig pivots to face her. She's still on one knee with her head bowed forward. It's clear to me she has information I don't. Silently cursing the years I spent rejecting all things magic, I glance at Belamey. He's enjoying the charade. Working hard to control his expression, he's refusing to look at me so I concentrate on Lord Bradig and Fin.

Lord Bradig removes a jewelled sword from a belt

that's hidden under the folds of his belly. "Finley Salinger, I mark you as friend to Lord Bradig, the superlative, and as such, we are now friends for life," he declares, tapping the blade of his sword lightly on each of her shoulders. "You may rise now in my presence and accept your duty as my friend."

Fin lifts her head and looks at him with one of her best smiles. She rises to her feet. "Thank you, Lord Bradig. My friends call me Fin."

"Fin, Fin," he punctuates with a series of hiccups. "I will call you Fin, the reverent. My friends call me Lord Bradig, the superlative, but you may call me Lord Bradig."

I'm aware the scene with Fin has ended. I'm the only unintroduced person. My mind is working through the options for not taking part in this spectacle. Fin and Belamey are already looking at me. Thankfully, Lord Bradig is fixated on securing his sword in its holder. Belamey's face is a mask of blankness as he watches. Fin, however, has widened her eyes and is gesturing wildly for me to lower myself to the ground.

I hesitate. I bow my head to hide my eye roll as I drop to one knee and focus on the ground. The tips of Lord Bradig's dirty long toes move into view, coupled with the smell of freshly tilled soil. I say nothing, mostly because I'm unsure what to say. He remains silent. Seconds pass, but I wait in my position. When his toes aren't in my line of sight, I lift my head enough to see that he has spun toward

Belamey.

"Where do you find such friends, Belamey, the eminent?" Lord Bradig asks. From the top of my vision, I see Belamey shrug and Lord Bradig nod. I drop my head before Lord Bradig returns to his scrutiny of me. "Raise your eyes, human, and address me, if you will," he commands.

I make a fast eye roll before lifting my head. I'm surprised by the squinty thin-angled eyes that are assessing me. They're luminescent orange, set above chubby cheeks, and a mouth and nose that are accentuated like the muzzle of a cat. I blink and nod my head again, briefly considering his aged face before I give a response. "Lord Bradig, I, too, am honoured to be in your supreme company."

Lord Bradig's hiccups have stopped for the moment while he continues to assess me. "This one is unworthy. I have decided it to be true," he declares to the room before he waves for Belamey to move closer. Lord Bradig pulls a very sharp-looking axe from his belt. "We must kill her."

I'm too stunned by Lord Bradig's statement to respond. My shock affords him enough time to hiccup and chortle. My eyes go wide as I watch him place his axe in his belt. He turns his head toward Belamey. "Shall I call her Kori, the doubtful?" he asks, but I don't hear what else he says because I'm distracted by this little creature's belt. I want to see what hides there. Instead, I note he's dressed in a velvet green long-sleeved shirt that has X-shaped stitching up the front, holding it shut. He has no pants, but the shirt is long enough that his belt has bunched it together to hang far enough to cover his genital area and rear end.

I can hear Belamey chuckling, "Always a joker, Lord Bradig."

Lord Bradig is suddenly hiccupping in my direction again. I keep my gaze down, trying patiently to wait out this spectacle. "I mark you as friend to Lord Bradig, the superlative, and as such, we are now friends for life." Then there's the light tapping of the sword blade on my shoulders. "You may rise now in my presence and accept your duty as my friend, Kori, the renowned."

I rise with a questioning guise. Lord Bradig sees it, and a look of pleasure pastes itself on his wrinkled features. "Yes, Kori, the renowned, Lord Bradig knows about Kori Ember and her family without being told and—"

"Why are you here, Lord Bradig?" Belamey interrupts.

"I bring a message from—" His head snaps to the front window. "Danger. We must leave."

"He isn't wrong." I hunt for a clue, focusing on the humans, or normies as we refer to them, walking down the street.

I pinch and knead the bridge of my nose when I realize the futility of normies regarding a tip-off. Spellbinders and normies live amongst one another, but most normies don't know about the world of magic that surrounds them, so they won't be able to provide any clues about what's approaching. Even if they sensed something odd, they'd rationalize it as a change in weather, a flu, or something that fits the scope of their sentience. Normies are conditioned not to see magic. There are exceptions. Rare normies whose conditioning fails might choose to see, but most remain blind to it. I don't know how the normies are conditioned. Maybe it's self-inflicted? Regardless, they grow up learning about magic but believe it's the stuff of stories, fairy tales, myths, and legends. They make sense of magical things they refuse to accept by explaining them away as superstition, coincidences, or with scientific reasoning. All I know is that they've always been conditioned.

I can't see danger outside the window, but I can feel something very unpleasant approaching fast. "Is the backdoor accessible?"

"Yes, but if the front isn't a safe exit, it won't be either." Fin winks at Belamey. "I have a plan."

Belamey shrugs, unconcerned, and gives a lead-the-way gesture. I ponder the front window before I follow them toward the kitchen. Fin is standing by a newly built-in bookshelf she had installed to hold cookbooks. On the other side of the kitchen, Lord Bradig is bouncing foot to foot in front of the exterior door. His hands rest on his axe and sword handles. A violent pull on the door sends a loud metallic bang echoing through the kitchen. Lord Bradig stops bouncing and arms himself with his axe and sword.

"Um, Fin? Your plan?" I lock my eyes on the exit. Given the level of force shaking the door, it wouldn't surprise me if it came off the hinges. I'm so busy watching the door that I don't notice Fin, but the bookshelf shifts, and there's a tunnel in front of us.

"In." Fin waves us forward. Belamey takes the lead when it's obvious that nobody else intends to. Lord Bradig and I follow.

"Fin," I say seeing an opportunity to speak to her without anyone hearing. "How did you know about Lord Bradig?"

Fin doesn't answer. I spin, thinking the worst. Fin dashes around the corner into the kitchen. It's seconds before she returns, and the door seals shut. "Don't worry, I had the door warded to keep it from detection and, of course, from unwanted entry," she whispers, trying to push me down the tunnel. I stand there staring at her with my mouth hanging open.

Fin scrunches her nose. "I wasn't the person to ward it, silly."

"Obviously," I say. Fin is one of those normies who can see magic. "That is the least of what I was thinking, Fin."

Fin pushes past me and forces a small, hard object into my chest. I grab it by reflex and look down. It's a well-read book. The scent of lavender clings to it so strongly it's like I'm standing in Grama Pearle's store. I recognize it as one of her books that she references as ancient knowledge. This book is called *Shapeshifters and Hybrids*. I don't question Fin; she loves books from Grama Pearle's bookshelf.

Belamey and Lord Bradig set a steady pace, and Fin is hurrying to catch up. I turn and start down the tunnel too. We don't go far before entering a small room with several closed doors. Fin closes our door and faces Belamey. "You don't remember which one, do you?"

"Nope," he shrugs.

Fin points to a door on Belamey's left. "That one."

I can't help but sigh as I look at the matching doors. *How could anyone remember what door leads where?* Belamey pops open the door that Fin identified, and he and Lord Bradig disappear through it. As soon as they're out of sight, Fin turns to me with a satisfied smirk.

"What?" I ask.

"This feels like old times, but with a new twist." Fin moves toward the door without waiting for me to answer.

"Fin?"

"Yes."

"Any other surprises?"

"One would assume," she says with a giggle.

I jump when the door automatically swings shut. When I turn to look at it, I question why I'm surprised that I don't see any visible ways to open it. With a shake of my head, I run up the stairs.

Snow is coming down in fluffy flakes, but the air is only cold enough to feel fresh against my skin. If we weren't being pursued, I would've been content to face the sky and feel the snow's tickle.

"Kori," Fin calls from across the parking lot.

We have exited the tunnel into the lot of the business down the street from Just Flavours. I look toward Fin's voice, and I see the lime green line on her Ford Bronco glistening under the snow.

The truck is idling with Fin in the driver's seat. Lord Bradig and Belamey have taken up positions inside the cab, which means I'll leave the parking lot sitting in the snow-filled box of the truck. With a humph, I climb over the tailgate. The truck slider window pops open, and one of them stuffs a blanket out before slamming the window shut again.

Fin doesn't check to see if I'm in a secure position before she rockets out of the lot. She goes in the opposite direction of Just Flavours on a street with enough traffic that snowy tire tracks won't be an issue. Nobody tracked our retreat, but there's no reason to let them get eyes on us. I grab the blanket, wrap myself as best I can, and nestle down against the truck floor to avoid the biting wind.

Chapter 2

Given Fin's comment about how our current circumstances feel to her like old times with a new twist, I'm not surprised when she drives straight to the safe house. Nothing about this ranch-style house has changed, including Daken and Galox, the two guard lion gargoyles, sitting at the front door. As we drive by them, both their heads turn in our direction. The corners of Galox's mouth retreat sluggishly as if she's trying to smile a greeting, but the effect is terrifying. The series of tiny spikes lining Galox's bottom jaw shift with her movement, and the melting snow and sunshine make each fang and spike look wet with blood. Daken's protruding eyes with vertical pupils follow us, but he gives only one long, animated blink of acknowledgement.

The vehicle rolls to a stop, and Fin jumps out so quickly that I wonder if she even put the vehicle in park. "I know this is one of the first places someone from The Society of the Blood Wind will look for us," Fin announces as soon as she opens the door to the truck. "But it's a warded and well guarded refuge making it a great location to figure out what's going on." She lifts her shoulders. "This haven just makes sense."

I shrug in response as I watch the porch. Deliberately, I draw in a long breath of air and steadily release it. The crisp winter air smells different in the country, absent of fast-food chains, extensive traffic, and various urban pollutants. My memory of the first time I saw this porch is fresh. I can almost see Birdie Ainsley, her less than five-foot frame posed on the top step, ready to do battle with whoever arrived uninvited. However, it's Talon, Birdie's son, who steps out onto the porch to greet us. His small stature, big round eyes, and bird-like mannerisms remind me so much of his mother that it reawakens an ache in my heart.

Talon says nothing as he looks us over. I know the surprised expression on his face is his regular resting face. He's approximately twenty-five years my senior, but his constantly shocked countenance makes him seem years younger. I watch his owlish eyes take in Lord Bradig, but Talon's only reaction is a thoughtful nod. With his eyes skyward, he scans, proficient in his inherited duties. With a flourish of his hand, Talon waves us into the house. When he opens the door the sounds of numerous chirping birds can be heard. His hooded grey robe sways as he hastens inside, leaving us to follow. We hurry in and close the door. I don't think we were tailed, but given we're unenlightened, the extra caution won't go amiss.

The screened-in sunroom is exactly as I remember. It's warm and tropical, a welcoming contrast after my winter ride in the open box of the truck. A botanical fragrance masks the musky, slightly dusty smell of the birds. Various types of local and exotic plants, decorative Buddhas, and an unknown number of bird species crowd the room. Even the aged dinner table still sits in the centre of the rectangular space, covered in smaller potted plants, water dishes, and bird food.

Talon is hopping on the spot. He's pumping Belamey's hand up and down like Belamey is a windup toy Talon is prepping to do a trick. With equal vigour, Talon releases Belamey's hand and literally hops to Fin, embracing her in a hug. Talon hops to me next, and I'm surprised by the strength of his embrace. When he releases me, he turns to Lord Bradig. My eyes involuntarily widen as Talon bows to him. I'm the only one who was ill-prepared to meet Lord Bradig. *What is his species?* I make a mental note to sift through *Shapeshifters and Hybrids*.

"Welcome to my sanctuary, Lord . . ." Talon stumbles, looking for a volunteer to fill in Lord Bradig's name.

The birds in the room have gone quiet as if they're aware of the honour Lord Bradig's presence dictates.

It's Lord Bradig himself who answers. "I am Lord Bradig, the superlative."

"Smoke and ashes," I mumble. I lace my fingers together tapping them against the back of my hands while I wait out the spectacle about to follow.

"Okay, folks," Talon says, and I'm sure his amplified voice is meant to redirect my ceiling perusal. "I'm happy to see each of you, but I know this isn't a social visit. So, what's going on?"

Fin hurries through an explanation of our morning's events, and when she finishes, everyone, except Belamey, is staring at Lord Bradig. Belamey's eyes cut sideways toward the porch. The scene with Lord Bradig is too distracting for me to give Belamey's behaviour much thought.

Lord Bradig has a pretty green and yellow parakeet perched on his arm. His oversized hand is gently stroking the bird's feathers. It's yellow head cocks to the side, watching Lord Bradig's face. He's making quiet chirping noises to the bird. As we continue to stare at them, the bird chatters with interspersed chirps and clicks. I close my eyes to keep them from coming completely out of my head.

"He talks to birds?" I whisper at Fin.

She hisses, "Read the book."

I shift my gaze to her, and I point. "This one is for you," I mouth and I roll my eyes. Fin smirks and winks at me before Lord Bradig becomes her focal point.

Several other birds have drifted toward him and

the parakeet. Each bird cocks its head to and fro, as if they are active listeners in a fascinating conversation. I note that Talon, Belamey, and Fin are also standing with their heads cocked to the side like active participants. Besides a peep at the clock, Belamey is fully engrossed in Lord Bradig's display of bird communication.

Feeling short-tempered, I stifle another eye roll. "Excuse me, Lord Bradig. I'm sorry to interrupt, but I'd hate to get attacked again before we're updated."

Every sound in the room has stopped. Everyone, including the birds, is now staring at me. I lower my chin to my chest and sigh. I creak an eye open and look at Talon. "Do you have coffee?"

Talon gives a hoot and hops toward the door leading to the kitchen. I don't bother looking at anybody else as I hurry after him. Talon has mugs, cream, and sugar set out on a serving tray like he was expecting somebody's arrival. The coffee has finished brewing, and the smell is rich. Scooping up the tray I carry it to the table leaving Talon to bring the twelve-cup pot. He plunks it down spattering drops of coffee. Puzzled, I raise my eyebrows.

He reads the question in my expression. "None for me just now, Kori."

I pour myself a cup enjoying the lightly caramelized and nutty smell of the hot mist. I feel my spirits rise, and I move the mug to my lips. Fin and Belamey come into the room. I sip the buttery, bitter java and wait while they get their own cups.

"Is Lord Bradig going to be joining us?" I ask once the coffee pot is deposited on the table.

Fin sits beside me and slopes her chair so it's balancing on the hind two legs, but says nothing. I'm hoping for a response from Belamey. He reclines against the counter and offers me a smile that would give me butterflies under different circumstances, but I'm too distracted by this morning's events to do more than purse my lips.

Belamey gives a deep chuckle. "He's just finishing his conversation." He turns toward Talon. "How are you, Talon? How's the safe house treating you?"

Talon hops backwards like Belamey's questions surprise him, and he loses his balance and plops down in the chair with a startled coo. Belamey's face morphs to one of concern, but Talon answers before any of us can ask him if he's okay.

"Busy!" Talon blurts out. "I'm busy, and this site is busy. Busy and busier." His wide eyes flit between us. "Oh, it's a good thing, to be sure. Rules of the shelter state I can't give any details, of course." He gives a guarded glance in Belamey's direction before he shifts his robe up enough to glimpse his watch.

"Of course," Belamey says.

"Talon, have we interrupted something?" I bob my chin toward his watch. "Company or, um, clients?"

He pulls his sleeve down and smooths the fabric. "Actually, yes, I'm afraid that my assistance is already dedicated." Talon lifts his hands, palms facing us, and he gives them a tiny shake. "You have a bit of time to determine what's happening, but if you require safe haven services beyond that, I'll have to refer you to another house. I do apologize." His big eyes dart from one of us to the other, and his facial expression takes on a look of surprised concern.

Fin rocks her chair down onto all four legs and reaches across the table. She clasps both of Talon's hands in her own. Without seeing her face, I know her eyes are expressive. "I'm the one who is sorry, Talon. It was my decision to bring us here and barge in without notice. We'll quickly be out of your way. I didn't mean to cause you any distress."

Lord Bradig parades into the room at that moment. He's smacking his lips and sucking air into his nostrils loudly. I'm terrified he's going to be chewing on the parakeet, but he proceeds past me and flips the lid of the coffee pot open. Upending the entire sugar and cream containers into the pot, he stirs it briefly. All the while, he's smacking and licking his lips. He closes the coffee pot, tips his head and positions it like he's going to pour himself a cup, but instead, he pours the contents directly into his mouth. When the pot is empty, he bangs his chest, burps, and starts hiccupping.

"Kori, your eyes," Fin hisses.

I swallow, crack my neck from left to right, and rub my temples.

"Excellent coffee," Lord Bradig hiccups. "Thank you, Talon, the keeper."

I open my eyes to see Talon dip his head to Lord

Bradig in acknowledgement.

"I learned great things about you, just now, from the birds." Lord Bradig is stroking his chin thoughtfully. "Great things, but that will be for us to discuss another time, my newest friend." He spins, looking for Belamey. "Belamey, the eminent, I come bearing an important message for you."

"Yes, thank you, Lord Bradig. We're ready to hear it when it pleases you to share."

My eye twitches. I don't know whom I want to shake more. Belamey for giving Lord Bradig leeway regarding when to share, or Lord Bradig for not sharing quickly. Talon must be harbouring us for thirty minutes now. I drop my elbows to the table so I can dip my head and use my thumbs to apply pressure to my temples more forcefully than my fingertips will allow. *Supercilious creature.* I hope that nobody will notice that I'm struggling to control my eye-rolling.

Lord Bradig's voice is quiet when he speaks next. "Cian, the protector, has sent me to you with a most important message."

When the silence stretches out, I lift my head. Lord Bradig has moved close to Belamey, and he's trying to get Belamey to bend down so the message can be whispered. Belamey is shaking his head no.

"Are you kidding me?" I blurt out before I can think better of it.

"Easy, Firecracker," Belamey says to me as Lord Bradig swivels and glowers. I contract my lips at

Belamey's use of his nickname for me. Lord Bradig blinks out of sight. I jump in my seat when he materializes, standing on the table so his nose is almost touching mine.

"Kori, the renowned, know this. It is only because we are friends that Lord Bradig, the superlative, is going to allow you to keep your tongue attached and not in this special box." He's waving a box that's suspiciously tongue-shaped. "A tongue secured in this box is for use only when I allow it."

My eyebrows shift up toward my hairline as I consider his threat, coupled with the fact that I know zero about this bumptious little creature. He's hiccupping so wildly now that I contemplate placing my hands on him to steady his bouncing before he jerks himself off the table. Wisely, I keep my hands to myself, and remain with my eyes locked on his. His hiccupping diminishes, but neither of us breaks the stare, even when Belamey talks.

"Lord Bradig, what Kori means is that we're all committed to the same cause. We were chased from Just Flavours together. It was Fin who saved us from the attack and brought us here to the lodgings of Kori's friend Talon." Belamey pauses for a minute. I fight the urge to break eye contact and look at him. "Lord Bradig, whatever message that Cian asked you to bring me, it's meant for Kori and Fin as well.

Lord Bradig leans in closer to me. He says nothing.

"Lord Bradig!" Belamey's voice is loud enough that it isn't quite a yell, but it isn't a regular volume, either.

"It's grand. It's grand, Belamey, the eminent," he says, finally looking away from me. "I was just noting how Kori, the renowned's amber eyes can glow. They are so much like my own that I feel we must be related."

Fin snorts and tries to cover it with a fake sneeze.

Lord Bradig, however, is not paying heed to her. He has transferred consideration to me and my eyes. My patience and our time are wearing thin, but how do I address this without him removing my tongue?

"Lord Bradig," Talon interjects. "I apologize, but this sanctuary and I have previous engagements. If your message is meant only for those here and must be spoken in the safety of this house, then I must ask you to share it quickly because I fear we won't be alone much longer." Talon sweeps his sleeve and is tapping on the glass of his watch face. His words have shifted into soft chirps.

"Chirp," Lord Bradig echoes. It comes out confused. I look at him. He's watching Talon. I assume he's trying to decipher Talon's bird noises, but Talon hasn't noticed the effect. He's stopped, but he's tapping his watch face like he's considering something.

"Lord Bradig?" I whisper. "Lord Bradig, Talon's chirping isn't meant to be spoken words. Talon often makes bird sounds as part of his human responses to things."

Lord Bradig and Talon look at me like I have lost my mind. Then they ignore me completely.

"Does that give you enough time, Lord Bradig?" Talon asks.

"I will make do, Talon, the keeper, and I wish you many happy lives." He gives a bow to Talon and then to Belamey.

My eyes are going extra wide and closing, a contrived effort, with a lengthy pause in the closed position. I see, in between my dramatic blinks, that Talon has turned to me but directs his words to Belamey and Fin after seeing my state.

"Go out the front door past Galox and Daken. Please leave in the Willys MB; four of you will fit better in it than in the Bronco. Fin, put your truck into the garage. Oh, and you will need to cloak yourselves."

When I get my blinking stabilized, I see gluey threads of magic. Talon is pushing and pulling enchanted gum between his hands and he's herding us toward the door. "We need four, Kori. Would you please . . ." Talon tips his head at my hands. He plops the stretchy substance into his mouth, leaving me to watch the gooey material being kneaded between my palms. There's no time for me to enjoy its flecks of shimmering colour. The gummy matter is soft and warm allowing me to knead fast while I listen to Lord Bradig.

"Cian, the protector, has sent me to you with a most important message," he repeats. "It is a find and fetch mission. Old magic has resurfaced. There is a woman who seeks the same item, and we must gain possession of it before her."

I plop the blob of magic gum into my mouth and begin the tasteless chewing stage. Talon has a bubble in his hands that he's manipulating over Fin's body with quick refined movements. She disappears, as does the bubble. The space where she was standing seconds before appears empty and, as expected, the expanse of the room is visible.

I watch Lord Bradig as I blow my bubble. He has produced a thumb drive from within his green shirt. "This has item details." He shifts his eyes from side to side. "I do not yet know what it is." He slips it into his clothes.

"Do you know anything else?" Fin's disembodied voice asks.

"I also have these." He produces airline tickets from a pocket.

Belamey reaches for them. He's standing tall with his shoulders stiff as I move toward him with his bubble of concealment.

"What kind of tickets?" I ask.

"Plane. The flight leaves in a few hours," he huffs with a glare at Lord Bradig. Then he focuses on my hands, moving over the surface of his body, fitting him into his bubble. "It's for all of us," he adds. The tone of his voice has changed. I stop and look up at him, not realizing that I've paused in a bent position in front of him with my hands high on his inner and outer thigh. His deep brown eyes are ignited with arousal. Heat rockets through me.

The front door creaks open. "We need to go to the

surveillance room to watch that," invisible Fin says from the doorway.

"The what?"

Fin is unresponsive, but I refrain from repeating myself because I don't know if she's there. When nobody else replies, I stand up and move my hands over Belamey's face, completing his concealment. The waves of heat coming off his body let me know he's moved closer. I freeze, not completely sure of where he is until his lips brush my ear. "Why are you still fighting us?"

I listen to his seductive chuckle that indicates he's distancing himself. *What am I waiting for?* I swallow and start to make the bubble to fit over Lord Bradig. The action is fast, given his size. Without conversation, I fit him with it.

"Someone's coming," Belamey announces from outside the front door. "I can't make out the birds, Talon. They're pretty distant."

Talon nods. Because of the bubble he's blowing to hide me his lips are locked in a pucker.

"Lord Bradig, if you are here, can you please follow Belamey? I'll be right behind you." When there's no response, I turn to face Talon. "Are you okay, Talon?" He fits me into my bubble. "You aren't in any danger, are you?"

"No, no, Kori. This is a regular part of my job." He withdraws to show that he's finished. "Good luck. Please send word, via bird, if there's anything that you need."

"Thanks, Talon." I hurry through the open door. Combing the sky, I see three birds on the horizon. Fin's Bronco is nowhere in sight. Daken and Galox, resting comfortably, ignore me as I rush toward the three-car garage. The Willys is parked inside by the spot closest to the man door. "I can't get in because I can't see where any of you are."

Fin giggles. "I love this."

"Please do not crush me, Kori, the renowned," Lord Bradig's voice comes from the rear passenger seat.

Fin is laughing full out, which confirms that she's the driver, as I expected.

"I'm in the front passenger's seat, Kori." I can hear a smile in Belamey's voice.

Fin's giggling stops. "It wouldn't be legal for you to sit on Belamey right now, Kori. But maybe there will be time for that later."

I skirt the Willys and climb in behind Fin. I deny my desire to swat at the driver's seat only because I don't want to hit invisible Fin in her eye when she's our driver. "Talon's clients were about to land when I came into the garage—"

"Did you see them?" Belamey asks before I finish my sentence.

Because we're invisible, he can't see the startled look on my face or the questionable way I cock my head. Without the other distractions, I can feel a tension radiating from him, and it doesn't fit our present situation. "No, why?" When he doesn't answer, I imagine his invisible shrug, and I replay events to see if I missed something.

We wait for a few minutes, giving Talon's clients privacy to get inside before Fin motors the Willys out. She drives leisurely down the gravel driveway, trying to avoid detection.

"It's good, my friend, that you didn't take Kori's tongue. I don't believe she would've been able to use the tongue box like the others before her. I don't think she could use it all," Belamey says once we're out of range from Talon's residence. There's no sign of tension in his voice now.

"Wait." Fin pulls the Willys over to the side of the road. "I want to see this box." There's a soft pop, and Fin appears in the driver's seat. Her head cranes to look toward Lord Bradig.

He pops his bubble, ending his concealment. In his hand is the tongue-shaped box he had earlier. Belamey and I pop our bubbles, and we all sit looking at the box. It has a rough surface with tiny bumps and veins.

"Inside?" Fin asks.

Lord Bradig does something to the underside of the tongue box. There's a faint click, and the box flips open from the tongue's tip. We all recoil. A grey-black tongue is wedged into the box. I can see thin hairs on it, with large papillae. As we look at it, the tip of the grey-black tongue flicks.

"Is that someone's tongue?" I'm not sure how I manage to speak because the moisture in my mouth has disappeared.

Lord Bradig closes the lid. "He's a wee sleeven, this one." He stuffs the tongue box into his shirt and pulls out another. "This is the one I should have shown you." He flips it open and it's empty. It's shaped perfectly for the dips and grooves of a human tongue. It appears to be moist inside and has a pinky-reddish hue. I sit blinking stupidly and moving my tongue in my mouth. Belamey has turned forward in his seat and is chuckling at my discomfort. I'm questioning my initial feeling of thankfulness about this box not having a tongue in it.

Fin eases the Willys off the shoulder of the road. "What happens with the tongues you put in the box?"

Lord Bradig shrugs. "I keep them and attach them to the owner when I need a spoken response."

"Why do you take tongues in the first place?" Belamey turns his head just enough to be able to see me in his periphery, giving me the distinct impression that he already knows the answer.

"To teach respect and silence, of course." He closes the box and stuffs it inside his shirt. "Sometimes the tongue is returned if the lesson is learned, but that is rare." He folds his arms up behind his head.

Fin flicks the radio on and I sag in my seat. I sneak a fast peek at Lord Bradig, wondering how much stuff he can hide in his shirt.

Chapter 3

We cruise past Just Flavours. There are no fresh footprints in the snow built up by the door. Nothing looks out of the ordinary, and I can't sense anything suspicious. We park in the same lot from a few hours ago. Sadly, our conversation about who might have attacked us is uneventful. Beyond the assumption that it has something to do with Lord Bradig's find and fetch mission, we're at a loss.

Lord Bradig's wild hiccupping as he gets out of the Willys draws me from my thoughts. I stand and stare at him for a few minutes with my eyebrows cresting my hairline. "Is everything okay, Lord Bradig?"

His body is bouncing up and down with the force of his hiccups. Fin and Belamey have joined me to wait for Lord Bradig's response.

"Foot-wise, which way do we go?" he asks in between hiccups.

I don't know what he's asking, and I'm thankful when Belamey answers. "To the front door of Just Flavours."

Lord Bradig claps his strange hands together and rubs them vigorously. "Follow me." Still rubbing his hands, he walks with determined steps. His body is arched slightly forward as he leads the way focusing intently on our destination. His arms drop to his sides, angled slightly behind him as if the rest of his body is going so quickly that his arms are being blown backwards.

I sigh inwardly as Fin, Belamey, and I take teeny steady steps in our attempt to not overtake Lord Bradig in his mission to reach Just Flavours first. His passion and determination are admirable, but his legs are so much shorter than our human ones that I'm sure anybody watching will conclude that we're intoxicated or out on a day pass from the local psychiatric ward. I'm smart enough to know that scooping him up to get us to the front door quicker will probably lead to me being stabbed with one of the sharp objects on his belt.

Fin slips her arm through mine, "I know what you're thinking, Kori, and I assure you that the insult to Lord Bradig's character would be a slight that only pain of death could absolve you from."

Fin's eyes are dancing with mischief as we take another small simultaneous step. She flashes me a big, toothy grin. She tightens her arm on mine and tugs me sideways into her, holding me close.

I realize that I'm smiling despite my growing impatience. "I think you're enjoying this a bit too much, Finley Salinger."

Lord Bradig has rounded the building. Belamey, Fin, and I wait a few seconds before we take a step together.

"Where did he go?" I hiss.

Fin is scanning the sidewalk, searching for our little companion. Belamey says nothing, but the corner of his mouth pulls up in a grin. Fin snaps her head toward Just Flavours. "Did you give him the keys?" she asks Belamey.

At Just Flavours, a few paces down the street, there's an elderly man supported by a cane. He's trying to insert keys into the lock on the café door.

"What in the blazing hell?" My voice is loud, and I draw glares from people passing by on the sidewalk.

"Lord Bradig is a shapeshifter," Fin reminds me. "You need to read that book I gave you." She releases my arm and struts toward the café.

Standing on the corner, I watch the old man disappear inside, followed by Belamey and Fin. I slip my hand in the pocket of my black studio pants, pulling out the pocket-sized book that Fin passed me earlier. I appraise the book for a second and then ram it into my pants. I lift my head high, regulate my breathing and then I march down the sidewalk and into Just Flavours, closing and locking the front door behind me.

Fin, Belamey, and Lord Bradig are nowhere to be

seen. A ripple of panic washes over me. Orbs of magic form on my fingertips by reflex, as I question if we underestimated the earlier attack. There's no noise and no movement. Then, without warning, there's a loud stomp, and a sharp pain radiates up my leg, starting from my big toe. I yelp in surprise as much as in agony, but before I have time to look at my feet, a wave of hiccupping fills the air, mixed with a wheezing laugh.

"Kori," Fin calls from the kitchen.

Lord Bradig's body is convulsing with hiccups and laughter. "I pity your diaphragm," I say as I hobble past him.

When I enter the kitchen, I don't see Fin. I consider the secret bookshelf door, but dismiss it. It would be open if they were in there. Lord Bradig is hiccupping his way up behind me. I clench my toes against my sandals and turn my inspection to the other side of the room. I know Fin and Belamey purchased the adjacent store to expand the kitchen and café seating area.

It's hard not to appreciate Fin's vision in this kitchen. It also makes me wonder if Just Flavours is a café or a restaurant. Regardless, the kitchen no longer has that industrial stainless steel blandness that it had before. Fin has imitated a kitchen from a rich person's home. The countertops are a mix of butcher block and marble set against vintage whitish-grey cabinetry. Four large gas-top stoves are set into the middle island, with a large prep space in between. Prep spaces and other restaurant-related kitchen appliances line the outside perimeter of the room. There are large doors on the wall to my right that lead into the oversized fridge and freezer.

Before I can take in any more of the kitchen renovations, Lord Bradig positions himself beside me and stops hiccupping. I look down at him. He's studying me with his unsettling, glowing eyes.

"Hey," Belamey's voice calls. I divert from Lord Bradig's stare and see Belamey with his head poking out of the industrial fridge. "Come on, Firecracker," he says and disappears inside.

"Lord Bradig, you knew where they were this whole time, didn't you?"

He gives a lone hiccup. I stifle my claustrophobic discomfort at walking into a fridge and closing the door, and follow Lord Bradig in. The clean, sharp, citrus smell of the kitchen is replaced by the stink of freon. The glare inside is overwhelmingly bright. I drop my head, squint, and focus on Lord Bradig's movement toward an open patch of wall that wouldn't be visible if the secret door was shut.

Blinking several times, I try to adjust to the change in lighting. I hear the door slide closed. When my eyes have regulated enough that my vision isn't blurry, I'm surprised to find a high-tech, windowless surveillance room with banks of computer monitors and fancy equipment. There are oversized comfy chairs encircling a small coffee table, and there's a tiny kitchenette with snacks, a bar fridge, and a coffeemaker.

Fin, Belamey, and Lord Bradig are framing a monitor and watching the screen. I note that this isn't a surprising space for Fin and Belamey. Then I'm surprised by a pang of jealousy. I stuff it aside with an internal eye roll. "Any hints on that thumb drive about who attacked us?" I walk toward the monitor, and move into the space beside Belamey. Instantly the delicious smell of cardamom, cedar, and lavender, with undertones of cinnamon, fills my nostrils, and I feel giddy. It takes a great effort to not lean into him and suck in a big whiff of his scent. *A couple that's not a couple, is that the label I want?* I blow out a frustrated sigh and work to focus on the video feed.

There is a picture of the cutest little animal on the screen. However, as I look closer, I realize this individual has several features that remind me of other mammals that I can identify by name, like the distinctive wrinkly shape of a gorilla's face but on a hamster-sized body. The problem is that all those features fit together onto this one beast, leaving me questioning its species. "Those have to be the biggest, roundest eyes I've ever seen, and the white encompassing them makes them stand out." I pause and search my brain for a species, but nothing registers. "What in the fiery blazes is that thing?"

"Our next mission." Fin spins in her chair to look at me. "And because of the unsuccessful attack earlier, we can presume it's someone else's mission, too. Who that someone is remains the question."

I blink once at the creature on the screen and shift my gaze to Fin and blink stupidly at her.

"And guess where we're going?" The excitement in her voice is energizing. "Costa Rica!" she sings, jumping out of her chair, grabbing hold of me, and spinning us in a circle. She lets go and dashes across the room. Fin has released me, so I'm facing Belamey instead of the screen.

"What's she talking about?" I ask him in an even voice.

Belamey reaches into his pocket and flashes the airline tickets.

"Belamey will finally get to see your skin," Fin says from wherever she is in the room. My eyes are wide as I snap them from the tickets to Belamey's face. He's holding a neutral expression, but I don't miss the way his eyes are dawdling on my body. I swallow, aware of a heat growing inside me under the weight of his eyes. "And you will see some of his, Kori." Fin suddenly gives a surprised gush of air, and races toward us. She slides to a stop beside Belamey. Her eyebrows do that suggestive dance that I know means something totally Fin is about to come out of her mouth. "Maybe you two can find a few minutes to relieve that sexual tension that hangs over us like a storm cloud." She smiles and bounces her shoulders up and down. "This is going to be fun." Suddenly, her lips touch my ear, her voice muffled. "He isn't Carter, and he isn't going to sleep with

Kinsley Ruen."

I can't look at Belamey, so I concentrate on the screen, forcing my thoughts to Cian. The man who watches, collects intelligence, recruits, and organizes our missions. Cian Caddel, The Recruiter, enlisted me and Fin, the only team normie, to join his secret crew. I know I shouldn't be surprised that he isn't here, but I can't help feeling displeased.

"Our first big job as the magic police." Fin occupies herself collecting pre-packed to-go bags for each of us.

Ignoring her, I spin, planning to direct my words at Belamey, but I see Lord Bradig as I turn. He's been so quiet I forgot he was in the room. Because he's the one who brought us the thumb drive, it seems reasonable that he has the information I want. I aim my demand at him. "Where is Cian?"

"You mean The Recruiter," Fin corrects.

I cut my eyes to her, give her a pointed glare, and then refocus on Lord Bradig.

"Cian, the protector, is—"

"The Recruiter is busy!" Belamey's voice is louder and more forceful than it needs to be, and I snap my head in his direction as I hear an almost protective note in his tone. Belamey is looking sideways at Lord Bradig, and his handsomeness is magnified by the intensity of his stare.

Lord Bradig hiccups. "It is as Belamey, the eminent, says. Cian, the protector, is," he gives a wild string of hiccups, "busy."

Fin drops bags at our feet, distracting me from my questions about Cian. I wave my hand at the screen. "Why Costa Rica? What is this thing? How and why is it a mission?"

"There hasn't been one in so long, Kori, the renowned," Lord Bradig says wistfully. "Cian, the protector, shared with me that the pieces of paper Belamey, the eminent, now holds, coupled with the map that Fin, the reverent, printed, will take us to the correct location."

"Map?" I spit the words out through my disbelief.

Fin is noiselessly clapping her hands. "It's a tutelary spirit that bonds to a subject giving said subject great powers. It advises, warns, defends, teaches, and it sees the true path." Fin heaves the strap of a backpack onto my shoulder and yanks my other arm toward the other strap. "If this creature bonds with the wrong person, the fate of the world, normie and Spellbinder, will be drastically altered."

"Where do you find time to read about this stuff?" I ask as she tows me across the room. "Wait." I yank free of her grip. "I need to go home to pack."

"No time," Fin says, grabbing my wrist. "This creature appears only at a time of urgent need. We need to get to the airport so we can find it first." She stops and aligns me with an award-winning Fin smile. "You're going to love what I packed for you."

"I can imagine." The bag is a lightweight against my back.

Fin propels me toward what looks like a solid brick

wall. I don't bat an eye when she opens a concealed door and drags me toward a waiting taxi big enough to fit four grown passengers. She pulls me in behind her. Belamey slides in beside me and closes the door. I look for Lord Bradig, but I don't see him. I jump when the front passenger door opens. The old man with the cane climbs in.

"Shapeshifter." The tickle of Belamey's breath on my earlobe reminds me of the proximity of his body, and all my other thoughts grind to a halt.

Chapter 4

The flight is over five hours long. I spend the time with my nose stuffed between the covers of *Shapeshifters and Hybrids*. The rough paper creates friction on my fingertips as I turn pages, a distraction that makes me rub my thumb against my other fingers. When we reach our hotel, which isn't very far from the airport, my body's achy, my eyes are tired, and my brain's struggling with the concept of reality.

Fin breaks through the fog of my brain. "This is completely unacceptable. I didn't fly all this way to not have a pool, a view, or easy beach access." She's spinning from one direction to the other, taking in our surroundings.

The plain cement building in front of us is four floors high with no visible balconies. The tropical plants in the hotel's front gardens indicate we aren't in Canada anymore. I can't name one of these plants, but their vibrant colours and unusual shapes are beautiful. "It works fine for me as long as there's a hot shower and a comfy bed."

My comment scandalizes Fin. She rants about suntans, stress breaks from work, and the importance of downtime.

"We are working, Fin!" I rub at my temples and try to ignore her while we wait for old man Lord Bradig and Belamey's shuttle. The air is muggy, and I focus on the different fragrances. There's a humid scent of ocean water mixed with tropical trees and flowers. The aroma itself has a calming effect. If Fin's still vocalizing her discontent, I've blocked her out as I enjoy the surroundings with all my senses.

The sound of a vehicle braking alerts me to the second shuttle. Stifling a yawn, I stretch my neck from side to side. Belamey and Lord Bradig, the old man, climb out. Belamey assesses Fin's apparent state of discontent and he gives me a knowing bark of laughter.

Distracted, Fin isn't up for the adventure of sharing a room with a male shapeshifter of sovereign status. Shockingly, she doesn't force or even suggest that Belamey and I share a room. Instead, she has powered up her cell phone and is walking ahead of us, mumbling to herself. She stops suddenly and wheels toward us. "What can I see from a second-storey window?" She scrunches her face up, twirls, and resumes walking down the hallway, scrolling her phone.

Fin scans open our door and tramps in. I get my foot in the door to keep myself from being locked out. Belamey chuckles. I cast a squinty-eyed stare at him.

"In the morning, bright and early." That is all I hear from him as I let the door slam shut.

I march straight into the bathroom and crank the hot water in the shower. When I come out, Fin's sitting on her bed, smiling at her phone. She looks visibly more relaxed, but I'm not interested in the details of her mood. "Night." I slide in between the sheets and pull a pillow over the top of my head.

I awake to the bed mattress springing up and down and I instantly know someone's straddling me and bouncing. My thoughts quickly appoint the title of "someone" to Fin. I flip the pillow off my head. "Smoke and ashes, Fin, get off me, you lunatic!"

Fin smiles one of her first-rate smiles. Unable to help myself, I whop her in the side with my other pillow. She topples over laughing and I scoot out of the bed.

"Get dressed, Kori. The Jeep will be here in a few minutes."

I sigh and pad into the bathroom. I left my bag in there the night before without having a look at the contents. Fin had strategically packed it so that my panties and tank top for sleeping were on the top. As I sift through the bag now, my left eye twitches. I pull out sheer pants that are meant to be worn poolside, a swimsuit cover, and a different-coloured pair of flimsy pants and I feel panic. I squeeze my eyes praying there's less revealing clothing in this bag. The bathroom door swings wide and I snap my eyes open, fixing them on Fin. She ignores my heated stare and picks up the clothes I pulled out of the bag.

"These are hardly appropriate for the rainforest, Kori. Think about bugs, snakes, and the sun. Plus, they won't go with the fun little hiking boots you have to wear." She's digging in my bag. "You didn't think you could hike in the rainforest wearing flip-flops, did you?" She goes quiet for a second. "Now, do you want me to leave these clothes on the counter or do you need me to help you dress too?" She winks and blows me a kiss as she reverses out of the bathroom.

There's no stopping the explosive sigh that comes out of me as I pick up a black tank top. It's so undersized I'm unsure I'll be able to get it on, but since Fin left with my bag, my other option is to wear only my bra. I wiggle and squirm to get the elastic-band shirt into place. Without looking in the mirror, I grab up the light taupe-coloured slacks. I'm surprised when I get them on because they're bell-bottom-type pants that are form-fitting on the top. They have a zipper, a button, and a cute belt, as well as two pockets highlighted with stitching. There's even one cargo pocket on my right thigh. I drag my eyes up from the pants and I'm equally astonished at how cute I look. Surprisingly, the tank top fits perfectly, accentuating my meager chest and flat stomach. The round band of material that acts like a collar keeps this tank top from looking too plain. My hand clamps over my mouth as realization dawns, if Fin knew how I felt about this outfit, she wouldn't let me hear the end of it. She'd be trying to dress me for the rest of our lives.

"Kori, the Jeep is here."

Fin thrusts a pair of black hiking boots at me. The new leather smell rushes up, offending my nostrils. I stuff my feet in, crushing the laces inside without tying them up. My feet instantly feel hot and trapped. I note while I'm still bent over that Fin has on more of an army boot than a hiker. The fact that I can see them makes me curious about her pants. I track my eyes up to see that she's wearing a pair of form-fitting pants that are a similar colour to mine, but she rolled hers up into capris and they don't have a belt or stitched pockets. I pause halfway to standing and gape at her. She has on a stretchy high collar shirt with a zipper, unzipped to emphasize she's bra less. I'm sure if she moves the wrong way, her breasts will pop out.

Laughing, she grabs me by the arm and drags me out the door. As we exit the front of the hotel, I notice two things. First, Belamey isn't dressed in his usual black cargo pants and t-shirt. He looks great wearing camo hiking pants and a perfectly fitting army green t-shirt. As an absurd distraction, I wonder if he'll tie his black boots for a change. The second thing that I notice is that Belamey is standing beside a Jeep, talking to a tall man whose chiselled back is evident through his loose-fitting, untucked shirt with rolled sleeves. This man's stance is familiar to me with feet spread, one arm hanging comfortably at his side and the other hand resting in the pocket of tan-coloured Bermuda shorts. He's oozing confidence. I'm studying him to figure out who he is when he turns. My eyes flash wide just briefly when I get a view of the scruffy, handsome face of Griffin. He wears his tan well.

Fin gives a little moan beside me. "Look at that chest." I can't help noting that only two or three middle buttons secure Griffin's shirt.

Griffin has an amused look on his face, and he gives that deep throaty chuckle of his. Fin launches herself at him. She's completely off the ground with her arms and legs enwrapping him. I catch snippets of his low, raw voice talking to her. Snail-like she detaches herself, and as she does, she flashes a sultry smile at me. "Griffin is our guide today."

I flick my eyes to Griffin. He gestures for us to get in the Jeep. "I have a network here and I know the area that we need to go into."

I give the Jeep a once over and feel thankful that the roof is on. The heat of this day is already apparent, and the sun is barely up. Air-conditioned travel will be welcome. I move to climb in but jump when Bradig fixes me with his squinty-angled eyes and high-arching eyebrows. He hiccups and laughs, clearly enjoying that he startled me.

I blink in greeting and slide into the Jeep beside him, enjoying the cooler air that licks the beads of moisture on my skin. "I suppose I shouldn't be surprised that you, Lord Bradig, know Griffin?"

"Griffin, the poised, is friend to Lord Bradig. Why should that surprise you?" There's an edge to his voice.

I stare at my feet, my voice is toneless. "Lord Bradig, I only meant that having just met you myself, I didn't realize that so many of the people I know had met you first."

He reaches into his pocket and pulls out a tongue box. "Belamey, the eminent, I must beg a favour of you."

Belamey turns in his seat. Lord Bradig thrusts the tongue box at him. "Please keep this safe for me." I can feel his squinty eyes staring at me, but I refuse to look at him.

Belamey and Griffin both give a bark of laughter. Belamey takes the tongue box and slips it into a cargo pocket. I cross my arms and fix my gaze out the window at the tropical scenery flying by. Shunning the conversation, I lose track of time.

There's a beautiful expanse of water visible over the treetops. I'm about to turn to ask about it when a yellow warning sign beside the road stops me. Never in my life have I seen this yellow and black sign marked with the silhouette of a crocodile and the words "Danger Crocodiles No Swimming." My mouth is hanging open as the hum of the tires shifts from a paved road to mud and gravel. The first rut that we hit in the road reminds me that my tongue is attached, but it likely won't be for long if I don't close my mouth.

The side of the road becomes thick with trees and grasses. There are still signs, but they're handmade, green wooden signs adorned with the yellow word Peligro and a crude depiction of a crocodile. The meaning isn't lost: danger. I watch the ground beside the road, wondering if I'll glimpse one of these deadly reptiles.

Griffin parks in a small dirt lot with limited cars. There's not a person in sight. Various forms of vegetation ring the lot and it takes a minute to see that there's a tiny well-worn foot trail leading into the foliage. I can't help searching the ground before I set my foot down. It's littered with dried wood and debris. I'm the only one with reservations about walking through a crocodile-filled environment. Everyone else is wandering toward the footpath. I hurry to catch up, but they've all disappeared onto the path when I cross the parking lot. I stop and blink stupidly at the oversized sign in the high grass. Someone marked the aged wood of this sign with white and yellow paint. The white capital letters read COCODRILOS and under it in a yellow, slightly smaller font, it reads

NO NADAR, NO ALIMENTAR. *Really? Do people need to be told not to swim or feed the crocodiles?* "Where are we going?" I breathe. "Hey," I yell. I run full speed down the path with a few hops and jumps when the grasses rustle unexpectedly.

I hear voices before I see people, and it takes all my strength to get myself stopped when I burst out of the path. The area before me is a short open space that leads straight into the water. I skid and flail my arms, trying to grind to a stop, which I do, but only barely. I swallow and scan the water's edge. It's calm and dark. There's a rickety-looking dock that goes out over the water. It has a few missing boards and no railings. At the end of the dock, a boat is moored. I'm hesitant to call this dirty white and blue thing a boat.

"Our transportation, Kori, the renowned." Lord Bradig's voice moves past me and I watch with eyes wide and an open mouth as he skips and jumps down the dock. The dock sways under the weight of his small stature. I swallow when he hops into the floating craft and waves for us to follow.

I turn to look at Fin, Griffin, and Belamey. Fighting an intense desire to try to calculate our combined weight, I notice for the first time that there's an additional man, likely the boat owner. The man has the audacity to smile at me when he speaks. "One at a time on the dock. Ladies first."

Fin has a small smile of uncertainty on her lips.

"I'll go first to steady the boat." Griffin moves past Fin, giving her a light tap on her bum. "Alejandro, I'm coming on board."

I feel frozen to the spot as I watch this muscled man step onto this questionable dock. One after another, everyone but me walks the gangplank. Because I'm not breathing, I can hear the creaks and groans of the dock with each person's steps. My eyes take in the floating craft, which I thought was low to the water when empty. It reminds me of an oversized kayak, equipped with a teeny motor. Six metal poles are holding up a thin piece of white wood erected to keep the sun from beating directly down on the passengers.

"Kori," Fin calls.

I gaze up and see that everyone except Alejandro, the boatman, is sitting in the floating craft. I'm surprised that half the seats face the bow and half face the stern. Alejandro is standing with a long pole in the water, trying to hold the boat steady while they wait for me. I swallow and don't move.

"Kori," Fin says again.

The grass behind me rustles. I rocket into motion and cross the dock in two giant leaps. The whole time I'm thinking, *I'm light as a feather.* My thoughts of safety aren't resolved when I hit the floating craft because my hurried movements have it rocking alarmingly. Alejandro moves his pole a bit, trying to control us. His skill with the pole amazes me, as does his patience when he turns to fix me with an *are you kidding me* look.

He shakes his head slightly before he directs me to

a seat facing the stern of the boat. The seats are two deep on each side, with a thin aisle in between. There are seven rows on the right and six on the left to allow for a small opening to board the craft. Alejandro has positioned each of us specifically for balance. I sit stone still in my blazing hot seat as he and Griffin pole us out into the middle of the water and start pushing us down the channel. I estimate the river is about forty feet wide, and I'm stunned that it isn't deeper. As the thought crosses my mind, the men secure the poles onto the craft. Alejandro fires up the outboard motor.

Even with the use of the motor, we aren't moving quickly. The channel is narrowing and the trees are forming a canopy over our heads. Between the tree trunks, the banks look wet. The perfume of the air is different here, a fresh musky smell of mud. Then I see them, more crocodiles than I want to count. They vary in size and have themselves pressed flat against the wet dirt. Their wide bodies are an interconnected pattern of scutes of various shapes and sizes. Most of these semiaquatic reptiles seem unconcerned with us, but a few lift their heads and a couple drag their hulking bodies into the water.

Deciding that it's in my best interest to shift my gaze from the water for a while, I notice movement in the trees. Small monkeys are hanging in the branches. I'm instantly captivated by their cute, pale faces and big, round eyes. My opinion changes quickly when one of the little baby faces sticks its tongue out at me. "You've got to be kidding."

Fin laughs and sticks out her tongue. I do a double take and then fix my eyes on Belamey. "Is this what I can expect from Cian's missions because—" I jump when a long, low-pitched growl suddenly fills the air, cutting off my words. Fin, tongue in her mouth, surveys, like me, to see where the sound is coming from.

"Howler monkey," Belamey explains. "It's telling us to stay away."

Examining the branches, I see only foliage. I cross my arms, but its intended display of emotions is lost because of my gradual movements. I'm fearful of capsizing our floating craft. "Are we almost to," I pause, realizing that I don't know where we're going, "the next leg of our journey?"

"Another thirty minutes." Alejandro turns off the motor, letting the boat glide forward on its wake. "The channel gets narrow and low."

I turn to look toward the bow, but change my mind when I feel us sway side to side. Alternately, I hold a static posture, my stare straight. I watch an unremarkable-looking bird swoop toward the water. The surface breaks as a gigantic crocodile breaches. Its substantial-scaled underside is a yellowish colour, but my wide eyes are stuck on the powerful jaws that snap closed devouring the unsuspecting bird. The tapered teeth latch on as the prehistoric creature sinks out of sight. I goggle at the now-empty space that the bird and crocodile vacated. My brain desperately tries to make sense of what I just witnessed while trying to ensure me that I'm safe. Instead, I lock on to the absurd image of the crocodile's massive upper body and unproportioned arms pinned flat to its sides as it came out of the water. To block it out, I close my eyes and take deliberate breaths until I feel us being propelled by poles.

The hull scrapes on the bottom of the channel. It's unsettling and I leave my eyes closed until the movement stops. When I open them, I'm thankful to see that I won't have to force myself onto the boards of a rickety dock. Alejandro has pulled the craft up to the bank. I scan for hungry reptiles but see none. I do note that the tree directly over us looks old and covered with a strange fungus.

"You first, Kori." Fin is eyeballing me like she's concerned with my blood pressure.

I don't argue but instantly wish I had because as I bend to duck under the boat roof, my foot kicks the side, making a bang. The strange fungus on the tree above us detaches and at least a hundred angry little bats take flight, winging around me. I have the presence of mind not to pitch myself out of the boat. I fling my arms toward my head. When the sound of my breathing isn't as prominent, I hear Lord Bradig's hiccups, Fin's laughter, and resonant chuckles. I suck a deep breath and step out with as much dignity as I can muster.

Chapter 5

Once we're all on the shore, Griffin pays Alejandro and we watch as he poles himself out into the channel. *Good luck.* I scan the surface of the dark waters. I hear my four companion's footfalls withdrawing but I'm not aware of their conversation until something Griffin says pricks my ears.

"Alejandro brought someone here before the sun went down?" I look at the water and the jungle, assessing the safety of our current situation in the daylight.

Griffin nods. "He couldn't tell me anything else besides she had fruit coloured hair, whatever that means. It was like his memory was blocked." Our little group has stopped as we consider the implications.

"Mind control?" Fin asks. "Ague?" She breaks the pronunciation of the name into two parts, Ah and g like the hard g sound in good, Ah-g and not Egg-you. At the mention of her name, I can see Dr. Ague Draven clearly in my mind. I shake my head and blink multiple times to clear the image of her dark hollow eyes and bright red melting lipstick on her ever-smiling lips.

Belamey is shaking his head. "No. Memory and mind control are Ague's thing, but just blocking a memory isn't her style."

Fin shivers beside me despite the heat. "No, Ague would have him dance like a puppet and recite a well-worded warning in the voice of Satan." She shivers again. In a quiet voice marked with fear and awe, she mumbles, "A psychological nightmare and magic genius all in one." I rub my hand on her back. I know that Fin's reliving Ague's temporary control of her body last year. "We're lucky that Ague is a good guy because she would make a terrifying enemy." Fin brushes my hand away. "I didn't think anyone had seen Ague in the last year?"

There's a collective shrug and everyone, except me, moves to the path. I feel like there's more to consider about Alejandro's mysterious passenger. Fin's voice is muffled, but what she says snaps me into the present. "Where are the horses?"

I flick my eyes toward Fin with my eyebrows raised. She mimes a kiss, making it clear that she asked about the horses for my benefit. Her face cracks into a big grin. "Horses, Kori."

Everyone stops and looks at me. I lift my

shoulders. "What? I love horses." Satisfied, they start walking up the trail into the rainforest. "They just don't always like me." I sigh and hurry to catch up.

In the forest, there's a small clearing with four horses and a grumpy-looking donkey. They're tied up and waiting for us. The donkey, with its short legs, is a hit with Lord Bradig and he climbs right up, eager to get moving. Griffin gives a wave after he climbs onto a big dark horse. Baffled, I turn to see who he's waving at. Nestled in the grass, there's a shack with an older man reclined in a chair. He looks to be asleep, so I'm surprised again when he returns Griffin's wave.

With a barely audible sigh, I put my foot in the stirrup of the only horse left and fling my leg over the saddle. Once I'm sure that I won't fall, I give the mare a little pat to acknowledge her patience with me. Fin, Belamey, Griffin, and even Bradig are already on the move and disappearing. I encourage my horse to follow, but she reverses instead. There certainly seems to be a series of events keeping me one step behind. Nothing I do convinces my horse to walk forward and join the rest of the group. I also can't get her to stop her backward movement.

"This is ridiculous," I tell my horse. When it's clear to me she doesn't care, I change tactics. "My horse is broken," I yell, hoping the old man will help. He doesn't move or answer. I roll my eyes at the timing of his nap just as a loud whistle fills the air. My horse perks her head and twitches her ears. The whistle sounds again, and she trots down the trail in the direction everyone else went. I shrug, give her a pat, and then just allow my body to fall into rhythm with her, happy that she seems to want to catch the group.

How Griffin's able to read the map while bouncing on horseback is a mystery. Since I'm the end rider of our group and he's the lead, I can't question him when he veers us off the main trail onto what looks like a path that a large jungle cat recently plowed into the undergrowth. Our pace lessens considerably, and it's hard not to be jumpy as branches and leaves slide over me. It's even harder not to panic when we stop completely, and I can't see why. My thoughts are filled with slithery reptiles, hungry predators, angry monkeys, and poisonous insects. We start forward again and stop. This happens a few times before I'm able to determine we're dismounting one at a time and leading our horses by foot.

When I reach the front of the line, I slide my hand down the mare's neck and slide off. "Good girl, Truco."

"Truco?" Fin is eyeing me. "Truco, as in the Spanish word for trick?"

I shrug and wave Fin forward so we can see what Griffin, Belamey, and Bradig are looking at. "Truco seems like an appropriate name, given that she started our journey together in reverse."

Fin laughs and moves ahead. We leave the horses and walk the rest of the way on foot. The foliage becomes thick as our path ends in front of a stone staircase. The stones are natural shapes built into the ground to make an unusual staircase. Green moss covers the walls on each side of the stairs. The stairs lead up to a small, circular hole engulfed with hanging vines. The vines are secured in a way that suggests human tampering.

My voice is barely audible when I speak. "Who in the blazing ashes is going in there?"

Waiting for an answer in the oppressive air is tiring, especially with no breeze. I give up trying to wipe the sweat off my forehead because no part of me is dry enough to succeed. Instead, I stand motionless and try to distract myself from the beads of sweat tickling my body. I watch Lord Bradig's bowed legs as he moves up the staircase alone. I'm still watching his legs and noting the permanent bend in his knees when he comes to a standstill at the top. His tiny frame standing there puts the actual size of the opening into perspective. Neither of the men nor Fin would have been able to fit inside. I might've been able to crawl in, but it would've been tight. Getting out would've been a challenge.

Lord Bradig turns to us and starts hiccupping. "Something is amiss Griffin, the poised."

My sweat stings my wide eyes, but I can't seem to stop my gaping stare. Lord Bradig's anatomy suddenly becomes a short-length snake with a moderately slender body. I can't see the colour or shape of his head because he's so high up. Between blinks, I focus on the stairs, planning how fast I can reach Truco if the snake comes down the steps. Nobody else seems bothered that our travelling companion is now a likely venomous snake.

"Aren't there jumping snakes in Costa Rica?" Fin asks.

"Blazing hell, Fin!" I shiver despite the heat.

"What? I'm just trying to make conversation while we wait."

"And you picked jumping snakes?" I fire back, never taking my eyes off the top of the stairs. I'm startled when Lord Bradig's oval head with long pointy ears pops into sight, but I'm thankful that he has shed his snake form.

He's hiccupping wildly as he starts down the stairs. "It's all arseways." He stops on a step that makes him almost eye-level with us. "The creature is gone."

Fin waves her arm at the surrounding forest. "I can't imagine it just went out for a leisurely stroll. Did it get eaten?"

Belamey's mind goes the same direction as mine, but he speaks first. "Any sign of a struggle?"

"This is typically not a creature that will struggle, Belamey, the eminent."

The eerie silence is a shroud over the forest. I sense that same unpleasant entity that we fled from at Just Flavours, but there's an intensity to it that floods me with fear. "Time to go, guys."

"Fast, Kori." Griffin's voice has an edge that doesn't

need explanation.

I run as fast as the environment will allow. The group is on my heels, the path too narrow to bypass me. My foot hits the stirrup and I fling myself into Truco's saddle. My trick-playing little mare wastes no time responding to my needs, and she's moving as quickly as she can down the trail toward the main path. I give her the lead and tuck myself low in the saddle.

"Left at the main trail," Griffin's magically placed whisper tickles my ear. I nod by reflex and prepare to direct Truco to the left, the opposite direction we entered the trail from. She seems to know, and she hits the trail and breaks into a full gallop. The other horse's hoofbeats thunder down the path behind me, but it isn't them that's causing the unsettling feeling of pursuit. Truco doesn't slacken her pace until a large, muddy clearing comes into sight.

Griffin gallops by us and halts some distance ahead. Satisfied with what he sees, he flicks his hand at us without turning in the saddle. I sigh as two dune buggies come into view. Just like before, there's nobody to be seen. I'm not fooled this time, though. Someone must be in the shed waiting to collect these horses, but I'm not interested enough to waste time investigating. The urgency to escape has faded, but I feel on edge.

Fin thrusts a cheetah-print bandana at me. She has one already tied over the bottom half of her face. I can't see her eyes behind her sunglasses, but I know she's loving this. Before I can tie my bandana on, Fin grabs me and tugs me toward a dune buggy. "The women are taking this one," she sings.

Griffin and Belamey don't seem surprised by Fin at all. She's picked the vehicle without the kid seat attached and Lord Bradig is already in the other dune buggy. I swallow double-checking the straps on my helmet. As my bandana and sunglasses fit in place, I jump into the passenger seat and secure my seatbelt. I can't sense anything besides the five of us and some jungle animals, but it doesn't mean we aren't being pursued, and the threat is outside the range of my senses.

Fin vibrates in the seat beside me and not because of the rumble from the dune buggy. She's filled with pure excitement, the creature and the unknown entity temporarily forgotten. She gives the dune buggy a shot of gas and we rocket forward. I'm sure I can hear her giggling over the roar of the engine.

Griffin is driving the dune buggy in front of us. "He's a perfect match for you," I yell, even though Fin can't hear me.

Fin is playing with the dune buggy. She has it tipped sideways. The passenger side rides along the side of the embankment. When she tires of that angle, she pulls us across the path to tip the opposite way. She aims for every large puddle-filled rut on the path and accelerates so we are airborne a few times as we speed over small hills.

We've put an enormous distance between

ourselves and the horses and even more space between us and the threat. I don't know if the empty ocean beach was part of the trail or if Griffin found it to provide a fast outlet for our stress release. Pressing into my seat, I brace as Fin performs several fast turns, kicking up the red sand of the beach. While she drives in and out of the ocean, I keep my eyes closed as the spray of water hits me. When she abandons the shoreline I sneak a peek and I see Griffin and Belamey switch seats. I'm surprised when Fin stops. Belamey, now in the driver's seat, seems to enjoy the dune buggy as much as Griffin and Fin.

Fin hollers at me. "You want to drive?"

I consider her offer, but shake my head no. She throws her arms up and dances in her seat before she slams her foot on the gas. I'm smiling under my bandana at my child-like friend. We head off the empty beach down a fresh trail.

Belamey pulls to the side and lets Fin take the lead. Shortly after, we pull onto the main roadway. Fin is driving now like we're a regular car in traffic. My jaw drops open and I immediately regret the action as my mouth coats with dust. I spit, but the grit clings to my mouth, crunching between my teeth. We haven't returned to our run-of-the-mill accommodations from last night.

I'm sitting in the parked dune buggy, staring at the sign that marks this as a hot spring, hotel, spa, and resort. It isn't until Fin comes to my side of the vehicle and pats me on the shoulder that the spell breaks. I climb out and pull off my helmet. I pop my sunglasses onto the top of my head and turn to Fin. My words die on my lips as I get a good look at her. Our drive coated her entire body in a blend of dust and mud. Dismayed, I scour the front of myself.

Fin grins like this is the best day of her life. "Booked this beauty last night. It'll be a great place for us to figure out what the creature's absence means and what to do about it." Seeing the skepticism on my face, she shrugs. "What? We've no idea where to look for it now. Besides," she says, breaking into a glowing grin, "sex will spark my creative problem-solving skills." She wiggles her eyebrows up and down.

Belamey, Griffin, and Lord Bradig, the old man, joins us. They, unquestionably, spent the last few hours rolling in the mud pit, too. I cringe. "We can't go inside like this."

Fin shrugs. "They're expecting us. I had our bags delivered to the front desk." She strolls away and the others follow.

I'm at a loss for words.

"Kori," Fin calls. "We need to get cleaned up and down to the hot springs. We have some important issues to discuss."

I inhale deeply and follow the group. By the time I get inside, there's no sign of Fin and Griffin. Lord Bradig is hovering over to the side, watching my approach with his eyes shifting between me and Belamey. I avoid eye contact as I take my last few steps toward them, knowing full well what Fin has done.

"Here you go, roomie." Belamey hands me my bag.

I peek at him. He's smirking and enjoying my discomfort.

"I'll shower in Lord Bradig's room so you can get cleaned up, but I have no plan to sleep there." His eyes run down the full length of my body and up, holding me like prey in a predator's gaze. I swallow. Not exactly a predator's gaze. The deep brown pools of his eyes reflect a different kind of hunger, one that makes my lady bits ache and I tremble in response. My mouth and brain won't formulate words. Belamey laughs and places his hand on the small of my back, ignoring the sparks of heat bouncing between us. He directs me toward our room.

"Fin wants us to meet in half an hour. She said there's a bar area where you can sit in the hot spring."

I nod and scan open the door. The bathroom is off the entrance. I won't go farther into the room because I don't need distractions. I know where my thoughts will go when I see just one bed. From the hallway, I do note that the room seems standard. However, this room has a balcony and great scenic views. With a sigh, I move into the bathroom. I drop my bag on the counter and turn the shower on. I stand, deciding if I should wear my clothes in or not. They're heavy with caked mud. Dropping them, I get in. The spray of the water feels like raindrops from heaven and I watch the red-brown water drain away with the day's dirt and sweat. My thoughts swirl with the missing creature, the mysterious boat passenger, and the possibility of their connection. When the water is running clean, I turn it off.

My eyes land on my bag and all thoughts of today's events stop as I remember Fin packed my clothing. I hold my breath while I rifle inside the bag for a swimsuit. I fish a bikini out of the bag. White isn't a colour I would have picked, but I know Fin picked it because it works nicely with my skin tone. The top is a halter that has a circle of white plastic clasping the material together between my breasts. It's cute. I'm not at all impressed with the bottoms. They're a white thong with the same circle positioned over the hip bones. I sigh and wrap myself in a towel. With an eye roll, I leave the room.

Downstairs, my companions are moving out of the main area to the stone paths outside. I hurry to catch up, consciously placing a hand on my towel so that it doesn't slide away. Once I'm close enough, I hear Griffin and Belamey locked in conversation about today's events. I notice Lord Bradig is nowhere to be seen, but before I can ask about him Fin winks at me and then scowls when she sees my towel. "We're going this way so we can sit in a hot spring with a view of the volcano." She flicks her hand up.

I almost trip at the sight of a very high mountain shaped like an upside-down cone. Clouds obscure the topmost section, which adds to its awe.

Fin hooks arms with me. "It's active."

"Excuse me?"

"It spits out lava rocks. I'm hoping we can see it from here when it gets dark." She uses the volcano as a distraction and, without warning, rips my towel away and tosses it in the bushes.

"Own it," she whispers. "You're gorgeous."

If there weren't witnesses, I might have killed her. Instead, I focus on how grateful I feel that Griffin and Belamey are walking in front of us. I evaluate our surroundings and block out Fin's babbling beside me, catching only occasional words like steam and sex. The resort decorated the pathways with stone benches and tropical plants. The warm air and flowers create an enjoyable sweet, floral perfume. Several hot pools have signs posted beside them with temperatures. We walk past a small pool that is literally boiling. I'm so busy staring at the bubbles breaking on the surface that I would've walked right into Belamey if Fin didn't have her arm hooked with mine.

I scrunch my face up in response to that unpleasant feeling, but it's so faint that I'm not sure if I'm imagining it. A bird comes into view. I identify it as a toucan because of its beak and colours. The fact that it's croaking at us is why we stopped. Fin uses her hold on my arm to guide my steps. "That's the noise they make to indicate danger."

I plant my feet so Fin can't pull me any farther. "There's a tiny tube attached to its leg."

Now that we have spotted the toucan, it stops squawking. I have no desire to move closer to it, and I'm thankful when Griffin does. I can't hear what he's saying, but he's talking softly to the bird as he pulls rolled papers out of the tube. Once he has the papers, he stops whispering. "Go," he tells the bird loudly, and it does, but that feeling remains.

"Only Cian knows we're here, right?" Fin crouches down idlily. "Let me see your sandal," she whispers out the side of her mouth.

I lift my foot. She slips my sandal off and stands lackadaisically, inspecting it. Then, without warning, she slaps it hard against the face of the hot pool sign. "Costa Rica has the strangest bugs. I swear that one had a human face."

Griffin, Belamey, and I are all staring at her. "Fin," I flick my head at the glass in her hand noting the molasses-like tang rising from it. "How many times have you been to the bar?"

Fin smiles and starts fanning herself with my sandal.

I'm mindful that feeling is gone as Griffin unrolls the note and reads the message out loud. "It's Adria Blaze your tracking. She's travelling to Canada. Your plane tickets home are at the front desk."

Chapter 6

It took me a bit of manoeuvring to get to the front desk without letting too many people, especially Belamey and Griffin, see my exposed butt cheeks. I position myself with a wall behind me while Griffin goes to the desk. It doesn't take long before he returns, opening an envelope. Fin reaches her hand out toward Griffin. "When's the flight?"

Griffin passes her the tickets and pulls a photograph out of the envelope.

"Tonight! The flight is tonight!" Fin is itching for a response. I hear the dissatisfaction in Fin's voice. "Cian is getting a call from me about this work schedule."

Belamey and Griffin are studying the photograph. Without moving my buttocks off the wall, I'm trying to see it, too. It's a picture of the posterior of a woman going through the airport here in Costa Rica. "Is that

Adria Blaze?" The photograph doesn't capture much we can use for identification. Adria appears to be a physically fit Caucasian woman with pinkish-red wavy hair. Something about her reminds me of someone, but I can't think of who.

"Guys, we need to head to the airport right away if we don't want to miss our flights." Fin elbows me and smiles. "Kori, why don't you lead us to our rooms?"

I wink at Fin and blow her a kiss, feeling happy she won't win this battle. "Follow me." Instantly, I feel that familiar but strange pressure all over my body as I shift into a hummingbird.

I take an extra second to hover at Fin's face level, enjoying her now pursed-lipped stare. Her hand comes up to swat at me, but I've got good at using my speed and manoeuvrability to my advantage. I twitter at her for a second and then zoom off toward our rooms. I realize I can't scan the room door open while I'm in hummingbird form, but shifting now will leave me standing in my swimsuit. I don't want to be my human self until I'm in the bathroom alone. So, I remain in bird form, waiting.

It isn't long before Belamey is strolling down the hall, smirking at me. Fin is a couple of steps behind, grinning from ear to ear. I reassess Belamey. He isn't smirking. It's more of a suggestive grin, which makes me think Fin has described my swimsuit to him. I have an intense urge to roll my human eyes, but I satisfy myself with front and back wing strokes instead.

"Have fun." Fin winks and scans her door open.

Belamey opens our room without a word, and I zoom in when it's cracked open enough for me to fly by. Instantly, a ripping pain encompasses my whole body. My brain rolls with confusion, and I feel the door brush against me as it crashes closed. There's a thick iron taste of blood in my mouth. I barely have time to register that someone has hit me with a magical assault forcing my body into human form when another orb slams into me. The sting of the forced shift washes over me in waves like electric volts that make me want to writhe, but I've been immobilized physically and magically.

I can feel, see, and hear. I'm defenseless and fighting panic as the door flies open behind me, shoving my useless body across the cold tile floor. Belamey races in. His muscled body propels him forward in a blur as he barrels down the hallway with his head down. I can see the threads of magic entangling him; a magic shield fitted over him like a body glove. Immobilizing orbs, like the one that hit me, cling to his hands. The colourless orbs are designed to avoid detection. The two assailants are already moving toward the open balcony door. They shift, soar off the balcony, and veer left out of sight before Belamey can let his orbs fly.

I watch, paralyzed, as he closes the balcony door and wards it to prevent any unexpected return guests. The door behind me somehow opens again, and Griffin, Fin, and Lord Bradig race in. Lord Bradig positions himself in front of me and holds his sword up like he's ready to die saving me. The others clear the room while I lay on the floor.

"Were they in your room, too?" Belamey asks once he's sure there are no magically concealed people or traps.

"No, but someone had been there." Fin eyes me. "Is she going to be okay?"

Lord Bradig tucks his sword in his belt and turns to me. His head snaps to look at the others. "This is a different representation of arseways." He turns and cocks his head while he looks me over.

My eye twitches, which I take as a good sign, but I can't move my body. I'm stuck on my stomach with my head turned to the side, giving me a direct line of sight at everyone. All my efforts to keep my thong hidden have gone to hell in one magic moment. One would think I'd adjust to random magic threats, but this is preposterous. I make a mental note to work on my magical risk assessments.

I focus on my twitching eye so I'm not focusing on the smile that cuts across Belamey's features or the look of appreciation on Griffin's face. Fin is looking from Belamey to me, and I can see her eyes flick over my exposed bottom. A look of satisfaction crosses her features before she casts her eyes to Belamey. "Isn't her ass great?"

Belamey is moving toward me in his predatory way. "Yeap."

My eye is twitching so badly now that my vision is

fuzzy. Through the blurring, I see a flare of magic on Belamey's fingertips, and I notice a warmness creeping into my limbs and moving up into my torso. He bends down and hauls me to my feet, crushing my body against his. The smell of him, a unique blend of forest and spice, overwhelms me, and I wish we were alone. "I can ask them to leave," he says so low in my ear that it's arguable he even spoke.

Fin drags her fingertip across my shoulders. "Sorry, my lust-filled friends, but there's no time for moments of stolen pleasure."

The shivering sensation that follows Fin's tickle clues my brain into the fact that I can feel and move my body. I push Belamey with wide eyes and try to scootch past him. He slaps my exposed butt cheek. I yelp and jump into the bathroom, closing the door. I lean into the mirror and take deep breaths as I look into my own eyes. *Belamey, delicious unconventional Belamey. Conventional isn't what you want for your life. Carter was conventional and look how that ended.*

"Kori, we gotta go," Fin calls through the door.

Pulling on the taupe bell bottoms and the black halter, I wonder when Fin had time to request they be cleaned and then returned. When I open the bathroom door, she thrusts my sandals and a sweater at me. I stuff the sweater into the bag and follow the group to the waiting airport shuttle.

It isn't until Belamey clasps hands with Griffin that I realize he isn't coming with us. I sneak a peek at Fin out of the corner of my eye and hurry toward

Griffin to give him a hug goodbye. I hustle onto the bus behind Belamey. He slides into the seat next to Lord Bradig, and I'm thankful because I feel self-conscious about the whole bare-ass situation.

Minutes later, Fin drops down beside me, silent. I reach over and pull her hand into mine. She looks at me, and we share a sad smile over her separation from Griffin. She slouches in her seat and closes her eyes. I turn to the window and watch the darkness deepen. I realize the night flight is going to be a gift.

Fin's first spoken words since we left Griffin hours ago happens as we're waiting in the customs line. "Isn't that Adam Hart?"

I look at the far booth. "Yeap."

Fin elbows my ribs. "Do you have any pull here anymore?"

"What?"

"Well, I was thinking maybe the cameras caught Adria coming into Canada?" Fin bounces her eyebrows up and down.

"I have no pull with Adam." I shift my eyes down the line of officers but don't recognize anybody. Fishing in my bag for my cell phone, I mentally run through a list of connections from my days as a police officer. It's early morning but not too early to send a text. I type in a fast request for help with a brief description of Adria, hit send, and drop my cell into my bag.

"And?" Fin nudges me again.

I sigh.

"We need to hurry and get Kori a coffee. She's miserable," Fin says to Belamey and Lord Bradig.

My bag vibrates. "Actually, we need to get Kori her bed for a few hours." I sigh once more, fishing for my phone, which wormed its way to the bottom of my bag in seconds. Yanking it out, I load up the new text and smile.

"What?" Fin's elbow misses my ribs this time because I expected her jab.

"Well, I should have some video for us to review later this afternoon. But I'm not doing a blazing thing until I get a hot shower and sleep." The stink from hours of travel clings to my wardrobe. "And my own clothes."

Fin's head is tipped to the side. "Do you ever miss it, Kori? Being a cop? I mean, the connections could be really helpful with these missions."

"No, no part of me regrets my decision to quit the police force." *Especially, after Carter and Kinsley's affair*, I add to myself. I turn aside. We clear customs quickly without talking about the hotel room attack, and we don't talk about it on the drive. The assumption is that it was connected to the creature and Adria. I play over it in my head while we drop

Belamey and Lord Bradig off, and I'm happy to stop thinking about it as I slide beneath the blankets in my bed.

Chapter 7

"Coffee's ready." Fin bellows. Apparently, this is her attempt to wake me up.

I lay in bed questioning my decision to live above Just Flavours with Fin as a roommate. Mumbling, I roll out of bed, pad into our modern kitchen, and plunk myself down at the breakfast bar where Fin has set my large steaming mug of coffee. I take a sip. Fin tries to thrust her phone between me and my mug while I'm trying to savour my coffee. I'm nowhere near awake enough for the image of Fin wearing a lime-coloured thong and a triangle bikini top arranged so that it covers her breasts just enough to be acceptable. My mouth full of hot, bitter coffee scalds its way down my throat. I cough and suck at the air. Once I've recovered from inhaling my coffee, I glare at Fin. With her head sideways, she's looking at the picture of herself.

"Burning brimstone, Fin, are you trying to kill me?"

She rips her eyes off her phone. "I look killer, I agree." Her gaze is on her phone, "I'm going to send this picture to Griffin. We didn't have as many special moments as I had planned for us in Costa Rica." She sighs. "He needs to come to visit. I might let Cian know that we need Griffin's help here . . ."

"Did you even sleep, Finley Salinger?"

"Do you think the lime compliments my eyes?" She fixes me with her electric green stare and holds her cell phone up beside her face with the snapshot of her in her tiny swimsuit.

I stretch and roll my shoulders. "Lovely, Fin, but did you sleep?"

"Sure," she says absently. She hits send on her phone and stuffs it in the pocket of her purposely paint-splattered jeans. "Come on, I called down to the café and ordered us some Turkish coffees with Mediterranean egg white breakfast sandwiches topped with roasted tomatoes."

"Ordered? Just Flavours is open?"

Fin stops and stares at me like I have seven heads. I shrug my shoulders. She puts her hands on her hips as I drink the last of my coffee and put my mug in the dishwasher. Fin is still standing, staring at me.

"What? Did you change the name to Just Flavour? Is that it?" She spins dramatically and marches out the door. "I take it that's a no," I holler after her with a smile; rarely do I get Fin riled.

When I get down to the sidewalk, she's smiling brightly and talking with a customer who just came out of the café. *So, it's open.* I slip past her and go inside and I stand there scratching my head. There isn't a soul in sight. Behind me Fin is saying goodbye to that customer; I note the large bag in the customer's arms. *Takeout. It's open for takeout.*

Fin sashays into the store and hooks arms with me. "Another satisfied customer."

I look to see if I missed anything, but the place is a ghost town. "Who is cooking and serving the takeout customers?"

Fin laughs as she pulls me forward. The smell of coffee gets increasingly stronger. The kitchen has a calm hum to it with just one person present, best described as gangly. If it wasn't for the hair, I would swear it was Dodo. Dodo, the boy Belamey took in to keep Nekane Adelgrief from corrupting. The boy who befriended my nephew and kept him safe from The Society of the Blood Wind. The last time I saw Dodo, just short of a year ago, he had long stringy hair. This boy has a shaved head that fades into a stylized yet unruly mop that is dyed blue at the tips.

"Morning," Fin chirps.

The boy turns and I feel my eyes go wide. The awkward boy with stylish hair is Dodo. There's no mistaking the dark, watchful eyes, pale skin, and sad mouth. He crosses the kitchen to us in a few long strides, awkward, but working toward confidence. I see a hint of Belamey's influence on this young man.

Not surprising, since Belamey has taken care of him for years. Fin steps forward to meet him and the two embrace in a warm hug.

Fin jostles Dodo out at arm's length. "Look at you, so handsome. The hair suits you, and I love the blue tips." She plucks at the coloured ends. I can't see Fin's face, but I know she's smiling her approval. Dodo's pale skin turns crimson and the corners of his mouth twitch. He drops his chin. Fin's hand shoots out and gently tips his chin up. "Oh no, young man, you own it!"

Fin steps aside. Dodo gives me a faltering smile, red still colouring his face. I smile reassuringly. "Good morning, Dodo." *Dodo, a boy with no last name.*

He tips his head up and down. "Morning, Kori."

With that, he turns to Fin. "Coffees and breakfast sandwiches are ready. Let me make sure the coffee is hot enough."

Dodo moves to the centre island where the coffees are sitting on a to-go tray. A red stream of magic flows smoothly from his fingertips onto the coffees. He picks the tray up and passes it to Fin with the food bag stacked on top. "Ready."

Fin takes the tray. "Thank you, Dodo."

I'm trying to control the surprise from registering on my face at the growth in Dodo's confidence in himself and his magic, but I know my eyes are wide and giving me away. Thankfully, Dodo doesn't notice. He moves toward whatever he's cooking on the stove.

"Let's do this, Kori." Fin advances toward the

freezers.

I sigh, not thrilled to be making my way through the freezer again. I follow, suppressing comments about going outside if I wanted to be frozen. "Hey, Fin." She doesn't stop, but I keep talking. "Isn't Dodo young to have a job where he's solo running a kitchen? Isn't he seventeen?"

Fin doesn't answer me until we're in the secret control room. "The boy makes killer coffee." She thrusts my coffee at me, a burning weight. "And don't be dramatic, Kori. Dodo will be eighteen soon, and you saw him. This has been good for his confidence and his magic. Besides, once we open for dine-in, he'll have a full staff."

I decide not to open the conversation about how Fin just made it sound like Dodo will lead the kitchen staff. "When will dine-in open?"

"Not until this threat is sorted out. We're technically ready now, but the last thing we need is a full café and enemies breaching the doorway." Fin's shrug suggests she's accepting this as a normal part of business.

"Hello, Fin, the reverent, and Kori, the renowned. I trust you are both well rested?"

I hadn't realized Lord Bradig was in the surveillance room. I smile at him and lift my coffee to my lips choking off all the things I want to address about Dodo's safety and everything else Fin just said. She gives me an eye roll and changes the topic. "Here is your hot grass water, Lord Bradig. This is a new recipe for us, so I hope it meets your standards."

"Grass water is not a hard recipe, Fin, the reverent, but I appreciate your concern."

"I got you a coffee, Belamey." Fin thrusts the tray into the air with the last coffee before she sets it down beside the computers. "Wait, where's Belamey?" Fin does a full rotation.

"Belamey, the eminent, dropped me off hours ago to wait while he went to . . ." Lord Bradig pauses, and it's hard to tell if he's covering for Belamey or struggling with a word.

Belamey strides into the room. His husky voice fills the space. "I'm right here." He nods to Lord Bradig.

I look at him questioningly. Belamey shifts his gaze to Fin, ignoring my look. "Is one of those for me?"

Fin points to the tray by the monitors. She dives her hand into the bag and pulls out breakfast sandwiches. As she tosses them at us, she doesn't say a word. She unwraps hers and chomps down in one fast movement. Her eyes close as she chews. "Let's do this." She plunks herself into a chair in front of the monitors.

I decide to not look at Belamey as I move to sit in a chair by Fin. I take control of the screen. Within minutes, I have the airport security feed up. I settle in my seat and unwrap my breakfast sandwich, which is warm in my hand. The sulphur smell of cooked egg whites blends with the earthy odour of tomatoes, spices, and melted cheese. My mouth waters a bit with the anticipation of my first bite.

Belamey is standing behind me. I'm thankful for the rich smell of my breakfast sandwich because it interferes with his scent and the effect it has on me. I chew listlessly and watch the monitor. My tastebuds fire with buttery, salty, zesty flavour. Fin crumples her wrapper and shoots a hoop in the garbage can with it. Satisfied, she plunks her feet up on the desk and tilts in her chair, taking a long swig of her coffee.

The first forty minutes of the video aren't helpful and even with fast forward, it's tedious. No longer engaged with the footage, Fin is talking to Lord Bradig about different recipes that he makes with fresh grass. Belamey pulls up a chair beside me and props his feet up, black boots loose and untied. Arms crossed, he watches the screen in silence.

A flicker of wavy red hair breaks the screen stalemate. I shift my face closer as Belamey drops his feet. It's Adria Blaze alone and not carrying anything. She turns and looks directly at the camera as if this is happening in real-time and she knows we're watching. Long lashes frame evil blue eyes as she winks. She knowingly reveals her teeth.

"Holy shit!" Fin stands abruptly and bumps me out of her way. She freezes the screen and zooms in. The woman is smiling with all her teeth at the camera, although smiling might not be the correct description because it looks more threatening than anything else.

"Blazing ashes, that's Kinsley Reun!" I stare dumbfounded at the screen. "How did I miss associating that raspberry-coloured hair with that Suzy Hot Crotch?" I feel my facial expression tighten; I shove my sleeves up trying to control the inferno building inside me.

"Kori, the renowned, you are mistaken. That is not Kinsley Reun or Suzy Hot Crotch. That is Adria—"

"Who is Kinsley Reun?" Belamey interrupts.

My eye starts to twitch, and I push my chair away from the monitor. I slam my fist into my opposite palm and apply force to each knuckle until it cracks.

"Kinsley is the woman that had an affair with Kori's ex-husband." Fin leans in closer to the monitor. "She looks great," she says, standing up. "Is the divorce finalized yet?"

Almost two years, since the affair and my separation from Carter, and my blood still boils about it. "Just," I say, my voice lower than a whisper.

"Carter? The penis guy? He was capable of having an affair?" Doubt fills Belamey's voice.

I push my fingers into my temples, and massage in firm circles. They're all looking at me. I keep my eyes closed and draw deep breaths. *This can't be happening.*

"Anyway, Adria Blaze is her legal name, but she has an arsenal of aliases. Cian and I have tracked her before. She's clever and vicious. Although she often works alone, she has a very dangerous team at her beck and call." Belamey's phone dings and he stops talking. My eyes are still closed, but I assume that he's reading a message on his phone.

Fin picks up Belamey's dropped thread of conversation. "Kinsley, I mean Adria, is a Spellbinder?"

Spellbinder? I never saw signs of her magic.

"A powerful one," Belamey answers, and it sounds like his head is tilted toward his phone.

My mind is playing catch-up. *I always see the thin tendrils of magic clinging to Belamey, which I assume is because of his magical strength—*

Belamey cuts into my musing, "When Adria was pretending to be Kinsley, you, Kori, were trying to live like a normie and had been rejecting magic by choice for so long that you weren't even consciously aware you were doing it. So, no, you wouldn't have seen signs of her magic because you were grossly negligent."

My mouth is hanging open as I stare at him, shocked by his ability to read my mind. There's amusement dancing on his features. I snap my mouth shut. *Okay, so maybe he's reading my facial expressions and not my mind. Either way, he's correct.* I shove my hands in my pockets and ignore the burning sensation of my ears.

"Okay, I buy that she's a powerful Spellbinder, I guess. She always presented as a bitch not to be messed with," Fin says. "So, she appears to be travelling alone here, and she doesn't have baggage. Wait. If her team is so dangerous, what happened when they attacked us in Costa Rica because it certainly doesn't fit the image you're selling?"

"What?" Belamey says. I open my eyes. Belamey is stuffing his phone into one of the cargo pockets on his pants. "Like I said, she works alone frequently. Odds are she didn't travel with anyone from her team. She probably used local for hire to see if we beat her to the talisman and to hinder us." He stands.

"Talisman? When did we start calling the creature a talisman? Wait, you're leaving? We haven't discussed the talisman or where it could be now." Fin's tone of surprise changes to one of distraction. "Talisman? Creature? We can't keep calling it that. It needs a name."

"Yes, I'm leaving. I'll send out feelers and see what I can turn up for tomorrow. Lord Bradig, can I drop you off at my place or do you want to come home with Dodo?" Belamey has positioned himself shutting off any conversation with Fin and me.

"I'll come now, Belamey, the eminent." Belamey strides out of the room keeping his eyes averted. "Until we meet again on the morrow, Fin, the reverent, and Kori, the renowned."

"Until we meet on the morrow," Fin responds.

My eyes follow Belamey as he leaves the room. I barely bob my head in response to Lord Bradig and I wait until he closes the door. "Something is strange, Fin."

"What?" She follows the direction of my eyes. Then her hand is on my back, rubbing it in small soothing circles. "I've noticed. Might be a new woman. Have you smelled Belamey? Are there any new scents clinging to him?"

I swat her hand away and scrunch my face up.

"What?" Fin shrugs. "He has such a unique, delicious smell. It has to be magically induced, right? No, that wouldn't make sense. I need to ask him where he buys his cologne . . ."

"Have I smelled him? What's the matter with you?"

"Well, I just thought maybe that normal delicious Belamey smell might have a feminine note if—"

"Stop. Just stop." I hold my hand in front of Fin's face for emphasis. "Who and how Belamey spends his time is his business. It's just . . ." I try to sort through the thoughts and feelings that Fin's new woman comment stirs in me. I stomp my foot. "I'm going home."

"Ah, sweetie, I'm sorry! I'll bring dinner up, comforting food."

I tramp through the freezer, leaving Fin to close up the control room and I keep my pace straight through the kitchen and out the front of the café. *Kinsley Reun is Adria Blaze and who knows who else? What does this mean?* My brain spins with unanswered questions as I open the door that leads to the upstairs apartment. I'm so distracted that I don't register the sound of feet thundering down the stairs or the dramatic difference when it becomes bird's wings. A series of loud caws startles me. There's barely time to protect my head with my arms as three crows fly past me in a rush of feathers and squawks.

I recover quickly and stare after two receding

birds. The third crow, bolder than the other two, shifts in the doorway. I get a glimpse of a fifteen-year-old girl with a purple pixie cut and a facial expression that suggests she's smelling something foul. She's dressed all in black. Before I can register anything further, she runs off. Her hand lingers in view long enough for me to see black fingernail polish on a middle finger that is stuck up in the air. She dresses it in a silver spiral ring that branches up her finger with green jewel-shaped leaves. The sound of her footfalls fade.

When I reach the top of the stairs, I find our door is open. I send wisps of magic into the apartment to feel for threats before I tiptoe inside armed with sound vibration orbs. Given my current mood, using these orbs to temporarily counteract the effects of gravity on a target would almost make me smile. The feelers provide an empty transmission and I allow my orbs to dissipate. The first thing I note is that there's one open window, likely the entry point for the birds. Beyond that, there's nothing out of place. If I hadn't come home, it's doubtful that we would have known anybody was in the apartment.

Fin surprises me when she bustles in only a few minutes after me with a bag of food and drops it on the counter. "Girl, we have things to talk about!"

"Yes, why was the window open?"

Fin stops unpacking the bags. "Why is your eye twitching? What did I miss?" She spins from one direction to the other, assessing the apartment.

Looking at me, she holds up a finger, and hastens to the door, locking it. She walks calmly back. "Now, stop freaking me out."

"You should close the window too, since that's how they got in. We won't talk about why you left the window open in the middle of winter!" Fin looks from me to the window and to me again. With a sigh, I close it. "I just about got knocked over by three very agitated crows coming out of our stairwell!"

Fin's body knives are suddenly in her hands. "The three crows? Like Tawny, Mayhem, and Blake, the three crows?"

"I assume, but it was Tawny, for sure." With a shrug, I flick my hand. "They're gone, though, so you don't need the knives."

The knives disappear as imperceptibly as they appeared. Fin moves to the bags and starts unpacking them again. I lift my nose and inhale deeply. "What is that tasty smell?"

"Feta dill chicken burgers with yam fries. It's fresh ground chicken, with shallots, feta, and spices. There's tzatziki and tomatoes with it on a whole grain bun. And there's a smoky chipotle dipping sauce for the yam fries."

"I like your idea of comfort food, Fin." I slide onto the empty stool beside her. "Dessert?"

Fin reaches into the last bag. "Mousse-filled strawberries and peanut butter fudge."

Without communicating, we both appreciate that we can set aside the last few hours of unpleasantness. There isn't any discussion that can't wait. We enjoy our meal in companionable silence.

Chapter 8

I'm showering when I hear Fin scream. Bolting from the bathroom, I take the shower curtain with me. I enter Fin's bedroom at a dead run, armed with sound vibration orbs and coated in a shield of magic. Coming to a screeching halt, I scan the room for threats. There's nothing obvious in sight. Fin is standing beside her bed. She isn't making a sound, but her body is vibrating. There's an unusual smell in the air, faint but noticeable.

"Fin?"

She turns toward me. Her face is bright red, and her expression is one that I've never seen on her before. Her eyebrows draw down, her nose scrunches up, and her eyes narrow. Aware that something else is going on, I release the hold on my magic. I stand there dripping a puddle on Fin's floor, watching her draw in very dramatic breaths of air.

"Fin, you look like an angry candy apple."

Her face contorts more, and her mouth opens, but no words come out. I clutch the shower curtain. As I take a few steps to the side so that I can see Fin's bed, her voice comes out strangled. "They pooped on my pillows."

I blink at her a few times, trying to process what she said. The unusual smell takes on meaning.

"They pooped on my pillows. My super-expensive, I-can't-believe-I-spent-that-much-money-on-pillows pillows." She's pointing at the bed and staring at me, but the red on her face is fading.

I eye her bed. The crows covered her pillows in worm-like dark green poops and splats of a whitish colour. *It looks like they invited friends in for a party.* I work my brain for a Fin-like response. "I read crows hold a grudge." I hold my breath, waiting for her to say something.

Fin cocks her head to the side with her eyes on me. "You think they shit all over my pillows because I clipped two of them in the wing over a year ago? I could have killed them if I wanted to." She stares at the pillows. "Maybe I should have," she mumbles.

"I'll get a couple of garbage bags for you." I move out of the room, leaving a trail of water.

"You realize that I'm going to have to sleep with you tonight, right, Kori?"

"Like hell," I holler.

It doesn't take us long to get Fin's bed sorted out, and I let her pick my best pillow to avoid her trying to cuddle in with me later in the night. I'm never sure what to expect with Fin, and I like the bed to myself. With a sigh, I plop myself down beside her on the sofa. Each of us has a bag of microwave popcorn and big plans to veg out watching television.

I have no sooner finished with the paper-crinkling opening of my bag when Fin curls her feet up so she's facing me. "Let's talk about Belamey." She pops a bunch of popcorn into her mouth.

I turn to the television. "I don't want to."

"Do you think he's loyal to," she pauses. "We need a name. The Society of the Blood Wind has a name. Why can't we have a name?"

I keep popping popcorn into my mouth without turning my head from the television, hoping Fin will let it go. She doesn't.

"I don't want to be a society. Nothing good will come of that." Her bag crinkles, and I can tell, without looking, that she's tossing popcorn pieces into the air and moving her mouth to catch them. "We know Cian as The Recruiter, which I suppose makes us the recruits, but that isn't cool enough."

I continue eating and focusing on the television.

"We're like a task force or a specialized unit, don't you think?" There's a soft tap on the side of my face as a piece of popcorn bounces off it. I turn my head to Fin. She throws another piece at me, and I snatch it out of the air with my mouth. "Now that's the energy this conversation needs, Kori."

I limit my response to a snort.

"I got it! We can call ourselves The Squad of Influence."

I time my blinks with each kernel that I eat.

Fin pings me on the forehead with another piece of popcorn. "Stop your incessant blinking. The Squad of Influence is a perfect name because we're a small group, and our work influences the world of magic." Her smile spreads across her face as she nods her head in confirmation of her name choice. "Okay, speaking of Belamey, is he loyal to The Squad of Influence?" Fin shifts into the sofa pillows and resumes cating.

I throw popcorn at her and mute the television. "I don't know what to think about Belamey lately." Fin is giving me a double thumbs up, like she's my over-enthusiastic therapist wanting more disclosure. "Something is different, though." I pop more popcorn into my mouth. I put the bag up to my face to look inside, signalling that I'm done talking.

Fin snatches the bag. "Do you think he would have gone through everything he did last year just to flip sides? His commitment to The Squad of Influence runs deep, I think. I mean, think about the mystery surrounding his mother's disappearance, how that forced his young life into the hands of Nekane and Dolion, and the brutal ways they tried to toughen him up . . . No, he chooses to work with Cian because The Recruiter fights the good fight." She watches me and chews for a few minutes. "I don't think he has a girlfriend, either. He's acting strange, but it's clear that he still wants a piece of you."

"Blazing hell, Fin. Can you give it a break?"

Fin dismisses me with a flick of her hand. "He's hiding stuff, though." Her gaze drifts to the ceiling as her mind works through options.

I unmute the television and put my feet up on the coffee table. Minutes tick by without Fin speaking. I'm getting into the show and forgetting about the details of the day.

"Belamey—"

"Do you want to talk about the three crows, Fin?"

"I—"

"Like, who do they work for? Who are they connected with, Adria, The Society of the Blood Wind, or maybe both? We haven't determined yet if Adria is working for someone. Or maybe we should discuss when you're going to replace your luxury pillows and what kind of budget you'll spend on them."

"Kori, that's just mean. Mean!" Fin stands up with a mock pout on her face. "If you didn't want to talk about Belamey, all you had to do was tell me. I need my beauty sleep, anyway. Plus, we have a full day of work ahead of us tomorrow trying to figure out our next steps in this find and fetch mission." Her pout changes to one of her brilliant smiles. "You know what just made sense to me, Kori? Reun. Remember Kinsley's insistence that Reun was pronounced Ruin? What a B-witch. Get it? A witch that's a bitch, a Bwitch. Anyway, good night, my little Smouldering Ember." Without another word, she saunters off to bed, giggling at her joke.

My eyes are wide, and I'm stuffing popcorn into my mouth so quickly that my cheeks are puffing up. I set the bag down and turn to the television.

I'm not sure what wakes me, the muted voices or the feeling of eyes on me. There's a kink in my neck and a general feeling of achiness in my body. I take a minute to realize that I fell asleep in the living room. Even if I had slept in bed, there's no preparation for the wrinkled face of Lord Bradig being just inches from mine. My eyes open, startling him. He hisses and jumps, causing the patches of red hair that stick straight out of his head to sway wildly. I shriek and mask myself. Lord Bradig, standing on the sofa, twists his head left and right, trying to find me. "Belamey, the eminent, Kori, the renowned, has disappeared herself."

I roll my eyes skyward. *Of course, Belamey is here.* "It's called masking," I huff.

"Kori, the renowned, is talking without a visible body."

"Smoke and ashes! This isn't a fun way to wake up!"

"Firecracker has a bed in the apartment, doesn't

she, Fin?" Belamey asks Fin loud enough that I understand the meaning of the question is for me. "Any time you need me to tuck you in Firecracker . . ." He lets the suggestion ride out on the tone of his voice.

I stomp through the kitchen toward my bedroom, thumping extra hard so everyone knows where I am without having to see me. The smell of coffee is strong, and I stifle the impulse to stomp back and grab one off the counter.

"Hurry, Kori. Belamey just got here with hot Turkish coffees—"

I slam my bedroom door before Fin finishes her sentence. I heave a sigh and lean against the door before I blink into sight. Looking down at the front of my body, I note my t-shirt, which is so thread-worn that my loose tank top is visible through it in places, and then there are my oversized track pants. Every bit of my athletic five-foot-three frame hides in this outfit. I give an eye roll and a head shake. *Nothing to be done for it now. If he saw me, he saw me.*

"We have loaded Mexican egg and cheese melts out here," Fin hollers.

I realize if I push aside the smell and thought of coffee, there's a cheesy egg and garlic aroma. My stomach responds with a gurgle of acknowledgement. I select black studio pants and a coconut-coloured sweater that hangs off the shoulder. Glancing in the mirror, I scrape my hands through my hair and catch it up in a messy ponytail before I pad out to the kitchen barefoot.

Fin shoves a coffee cup and sandwich at me. I admire the grill marks on the bread, noting the sandwich's warmth. The orange of the cheese is slightly coloured with the brighter oranges of the salsa. The current priority for everyone is breakfast, so I join them to eat in silence.

"Will Kori, the renowned, be staying visible for the rest of the morning?"

I cast my eyes to Lord Bradig and consider asking him why he doesn't like it when people disappear on him, but his thin, squinty eyes are even more narrow as he assesses me. He's patting his pocket. I'm undecided if it's my imagination or if there's a shape of a tongue under his hand. I decide to keep my comment to myself. Instead, I take the last bite of my sandwich and nod. He relaxes his eyes. "Excellent, because Lord Bradig, the superlative, only likes to play hide and seek in situations where it makes humans scream and piss themselves." He hiccups wildly with both hands on his belly like he's a tiny frightening Santa ho, ho, ho-ing.

Fin interrupts with dramatic finger-sucking noises as she cleans the grease off her fingers with her mouth. "So, Belamey has reason to believe that the crows, or at least one of them, work for Adria now." She cuts her eyes to him. "But he won't tell me how he came by this belief."

Belamey shrugs. "Not important information, Fin. What's important is Adria is clearly looking for the talisman too."

"Stop!" Fin says, holding up her hand. "We can't keep calling it the creature or the talisman. I've named it Chimmi. Like Jimmy, but Chimmi." She makes an exasperated sigh as we stare at her in silence. "Besides being a creature and a talisman, Chimmi is also a chimera. You saw it! Chimmi is a blend of different animals."

I'm unconvinced that she has the definition of chimera correct, but it isn't worth the challenge. I dismiss it and move on. "Are you saying that Adria is part of The Society of the Blood Wind?" I ask.

Fin's head is wagging. "Nope, Belamey's source is adamant that Adria and The Society of the Blood Wind will never work together."

I direct my question at Belamey. "Adria has her own society?"

He doesn't even try to answer. Fin jumps right in. "Nope, she's a solo crazy bitch that thinks she can take on the world. She has a specialized team that she retains. The best of the best kind of team, but they're in her employ. She's basically a female version of Belamey's deceased father, Nekane Adelgrief. Belamey's source says that Nekane let Adria live because he liked the challenge she presented. It isn't clear if he wanted to raise her as a daughter or fu—"

"Fin," I interrupt. "I get it. Okay, so we know Adria is searching for the talisman—"

"Chimmi." She coughs into her hand.

I ignore her. "Do we know if The Society of the

Blood Wind is at play?" I'm looking at Fin, expecting her to continue being Belamey's voice, but she's eyeballing him. I look and he's staring at the screen of his phone. We both watch him in silence as he types in a message. His fingers lag, and he raises his eyes with the realization that we're waiting on him for an answer.

His phone dings, making him jump. I feel the muscles of my face tighten watching his discomfort grow as he fights to not look at his phone screen. He's focusing on Fin and won't look at me. "Ask it again."

"Kori, the beautiful woman with whom you're infatuated," Fin hitches her thumb in my direction, but Belamey's stare remains on Fin, "has asked if The Society of the Blood Wind is looking for Chimmi, too."

Belamey's phone dings again. His eyes jump quickly to me and then to Fin. "No."

"How can you be certain?" I ask.

"I just am."

"Is it your secret source, Belamey?" Fin raises her eyebrows at the phone clutched in his hand.

He looks at it like he wishes it would disappear. He fixes Fin with a slightly less defined expression. "Lord Bradig, it's time. Fin, my grandfather—"

"Dolion Adelgrief," she interrupts.

"Dolion is very ill. Any play The Society of the Blood Wind is or isn't planning is low priority while he prepares Kyson to take over for him. I don't believe The Society of the Blood Wind knows the . . . I mean, I don't think they know Chimmi is in play. As for

Adria, if Dolion knew she was this close to home, he would kill her even if it ended him."

I'm still shivering at the mention of Kyson Adelgrief when Belamey stands abruptly. Involuntary, my hand covers the scar Kyson's identical twin brother, Kieran, gave me when he stuck his filleting knife into my lower abdomen over a year ago. Both of them are evil Spellbinders. Belamey's arm grips my waist, pulling me against him, and his lips brush mine with intense heat. He takes a deep inhale of my hair and stalks out of the apartment with Lord Bradig on his heels, leaving me standing there, blinking and savouring the fading heat on my lips and the tickle it caused lower down. The blended smell of earth, cardamom, cedar, and lavender, with undertones of cinnamon and vanilla, lingers in my nasal passage. I momentarily lose control of my senses. Fin yelling at the closed door breaks the spell.

"Her? Her who?"

The sound of her voice is jarring, and I want it to stop. "Fin?"

She brushes past me and rushes to the window. Throwing it open, she leans out. "Her who?"

"Fin?"

"Who is she?"

"FIN!"

Fin pops in and slams the window shut. "I want to know the secret, Kori. I want to know who she is."

"She? What are you talking about?"

Fin purses her lips, puts her hands on her hips,

and raises her eyebrows. "Seriously, one kiss and you're lost to the world."

Now it's my turn. My eyes fly wide, and I stomp my foot. "Blazing ashes, Fin, that's fresh, coming from you." I take some audible breaths through my nose. "Now, what are you on about with this she thing?"

Fin relaxes and moves into the kitchen. "Well, as they were going out, Lord Bradig asked Belamey if it was time for her to meet him, Lord Bradig, the superlative. I didn't hear the rest." Fin's phone dings on the counter. She looks me up and down before she moves toward it. "He's too into you for it to be another woman. And then there was the kiss. But he's acting so strange. And, well, how long can you be a couple with one reluctant participant? You're interested, you're not, I mean if you can't figure it out . . . How long should he wait? What else could it be, for a 'her' to be causing him such discomfort—"

She cuts herself off with a shriek that makes me cover my ears. "Griffin is coming." She jumps up and down like a schoolgirl. "My Griffin is coming. Cian rerouted him to help us with Chimmi."

That announcement officially ends any kind of conversation with Fin. I shake my head at the classic abrupt Fin shift from one mood and action to another. How she doesn't give herself and all of us whiplash, I'll never understand. She races from the room, mumbling about new pillows, fresh sheets, and sexy pyjamas.

I spend the day trying to find information on

Spellbinder history and old historical sites in town. Regular computer searches are useless, I can't find anything Spellbinder related. I wish that Grama Pearle was home from her vacation. Her memory-keeper skills might have something useful stored away. Although I possess the same skill to store other people's memories like they're my own, there's nothing in my memory bank except a few memories shared in confidence. I do come up with a few locations that might be ideal for Chimmi to hide.

Between my unsuccessful day of research and watching Fin's endless trips to her room with candles, wine glasses, and numerous other items, I feel exhausted. I don't bother saying goodnight. I just sneak off to bed.

Chapter 9

Giggles and moaning break through my sleep-filled brain. I blow out a sigh of exasperation and smash the pillow down over my head, but it's useless. Fin is so loud. I slide out of bed and into my regular outfit. The world outside my window is snowy treetops, so although I refuse to wear socks, I pull a zippered sweater on. I stop at the doorway. The sounds of Fin's giggles and Griffin's groans are almost drowned out because someone is turning the television up at a steady pace.

I mask myself and slip out of my room on tiptoe. The first thing I see is Lord Bradig. He's laying flat, trying to look under the crack at the bottom of Fin's bedroom door. His body bounces up and down with the force of his hiccups, and the effect causes the side of his head to bang off the floor with each jarring vibration. Unfazed, but clearly disgruntled with his inability to keep his head firmly on the floor, he shifts positions.

My eyes go wide and they burn. My body blinks into focus and I slam my hands over my eyes with a stifled shriek, but despite myself, I peek between my fingers. Lord Bradig's repositioning brought his short frame into a downward dog position. He's using the weight of his body to keep his head on the ground when he hiccups. My positioning gives me an eyeful of what lies under his short green shirt. Two of the roundest, plumpest butt cheeks I've ever seen are up in the air. I can't look away. Right in the centre of each cheek are two perfect circles of turquoise, like a clown has painted Lord Bradig's bottom. The turquoise colour stands out brilliantly against his blue-grey skin. And if that isn't bad enough, hanging down between his legs is a turquoise penis that defies the odds of his body size. I cock my head to the side, trying to figure out how he keeps it hidden in his short tunic. *Blazing hell, I'm Grama Pearle.* I snap my head straight, tear my eyes from Lord Bradig, and spin toward the living room and the blaring television.

Belamey is sitting on the sofa with his feet up and a coffee in hand. He takes a sip, watching me. "Morning, Firecracker. Did you like the view?" I look toward Lord Bradig with his parts still up in the air. Rubbing furiously, I grind my fingers into my eyes. "Bet you've never seen one like that?" He smirks.

I swallow. There are no words. I jump when Lord

Bradig speaks from beside me. "Kori, the renowned, what is the sex? Belamey, the eminent, says that is what is happening in that room, but he won't tell me anything more."

My head snaps in the downward direction of Lord Bradig so quickly that it takes my eyes a second to catch up. No words come out. I look at him and blink.

Lord Bradig nods at me, coming to a conclusion. He looks to Belamey. "As I expected, Kori, the renowned hasn't had the sex, Belamey, the eminent. I will have to wait and ask Fin, the reverent. That is probably better anyway, because she sounds very good at it."

Belamey has turned the television down and, as if on cue, Fin comes out of the bedroom. She sashays toward us, smiling from ear to ear. "What's the matter with her?" Fin flicks her head at me, but she directs her question at Belamey.

Belamey grins. "She saw Lord Bradig's junk."

"Lord Bradig, the superlative has no 'junk.' We will need to speak of what this junk is, Belamey, the eminent. But first, Fin, the reverent, what is the sex and can you teach it to me?"

Fin turns her beaming smile at Lord Bradig, not the least unsettled. She bows her head slightly. "What an honour, Lord Bradig—"

"Fin," I hiss out the corner of my mouth. "It's enormous and turquoise." I ram my finger into my twitching eye.

She doesn't even shift her focus to me. "I know. I've

seen it."

"Say what?" I blurt.

"*Shapeshifters and Hybrids*, Kori. Did you even read it? Wait? Where did you think I'd seen it. Should I be insulted here?"

Lord Bradig turns to face me, stretches his twenty-inch height up prouder than his normal stance, and reaches under the bottom of his shirt toward it. "You want to see my," his face pinches up as he struggles with his questioning. "What is it you call it? Penis. You want to see my penis? It glows when I—"

"Stop," I yelp.

Fin leans down and directs Bradig's hand out from under his shirt. "First, an explanation about 'the sex,' or just 'sex,' as we call it. I don't believe you need a teacher." She straightens and smiles at Griffin as he strolls into the room and grabs a coffee from the tray by Belamey's feet. "Sex is what Lord Bradig calls whoopee." She dances her eyebrows at him.

Lord Bradig's hiccups come out so violently that his whole body comes off the floor. He slaps his leg and lets out a fart. A miasma of acrid mouldy hay pervades the room. "Fin, the reverent, you are my favourite human." Reaching under his shirt, he adjusts himself. I have a moment of fear that he's going to pull it out to discuss its function, but he releases it and continues his dialogue. "You are very right Fin, the reverent. Lord Bradig, the superlative, doesn't need a teacher." His eyes scan her up and down. "You would be inadequately prepared to whoopee with Lord Bradig, the superlative."

I can see Fin considering the implications of that statement, and I close my eyes to wait for her response.

"Alas, Lord Bradig, you are correct. My vagina wouldn't respond to the glow."

I choke on my inhalation of air. Everyone ignores me as they move on to proper greetings. Fin stuffs a coffee into my hand and rubs my back. "It really glows?" I whisper to her now that the crisis with Lord Bradig and his penis is over.

She nods without looking in my direction. "That's not all it can do." She casts a furtive glance at me. "You didn't read *Shapeshifters and Hybrids* very closely, did you?"

"I'm not much of a reader."

Fin's smile takes on a mischievous twist and her eyes twinkle. "Perhaps you aren't much of a reader, but you must be feeling some sexual arousal?" She makes kisses at me as she leans in close. "When was the last time you made whoopee?" she asks with a pointed look in Belamey's direction.

The nerve endings in my lady bits are the first to weigh in on the conversation. My mouth goes dry as my brain fills with lustful thoughts. I'm staring at Belamey and blinking stupidly. Thankfully, Fin's next comment pulls me out of my daydream before he notices.

"It's been almost two years since Carter," Fin's voice is scolding, like the time frame is unacceptably long. My eyes bulge when she starts swaying her hips in circles. "Belamey's been here for a year, and he's hot to trot for what you got!"

There's a suggestive chuckle from Belamey. Before I can give her a blast of shit, there's a tapping sound on the window beside the sofa.

There's a bird perching on the sill. Its black feathers look almost purple in the sunlight. Its black beak taps the window once more. A bird we can't see gives ten clear whistles. The crow jerks its head from side to side, its blue eyes searching. As we watch, the crow's right foot shifts into a human hand and, with practised skill, detaches a note tube from its leg. The hand shifts into a bird's foot. We hear the same bird song and seconds later the orangish-red breast of a robin soars by the widow. The crow watches the robin for a second and then it flies off. I don't know any Spellbinders that shift into a robin. A fast look at Fin tells me she doesn't either. However, we all know the three crows. The messenger was one of them.

Nobody moves right away as we all stare outside. My eyes stay glued to the window when I break the silence. "I think that was Tawny."

"I think so, too," Fin says.

"Why?" Griffin asks. I pull my eyes from the window and look at him.

Fin crosses her arms and straightens her spine. "Well, as an expert on Spellbinders and birds, I can say that Alivia's sketchbook documents which Spellbinders can shift into what birds. Alivia's description of Tawny included the mention of a unique ring worn on her middle finger, the same ring that we just saw on the messenger crow."

"First, I'm not sure if studying Alivia's sketchbook makes you an expert. And second, the other day, when I inadvertently stumbled upon the crows leaving our apartment, Tawny shifted into human form. She was a blur running away, but her hand held in place in the open doorway long enough to give the mid-finger salute decorated with that spiral ring," I add.

"It looks like a silver tree with beautiful green leaves. I need to ask her where she got it." Fin is thoughtful for a moment before she turns to Belamey, who has remained quiet and unmoving since the crow first tapped on the window. The look on his face is tense. "You know the crows better than the rest of us, Belamey. Are we wrong, or is it Tawny?"

Belamey shifts on the sofa like he can't find a comfortable spot. He eyes Fin, me, and the window. He draws his eyebrows together, and he has a tight-lipped smile when he answers. "That was Tawny's ring."

The tightness in my chest loosens, I hadn't realized I was holding my breath. I set my coffee down, and move toward the window. "Anyone expecting a message?" I push the window open and pick the small tube up, my eyes scanning the skies. Satisfied that no other birds are waiting, I close the window.

Assuming that the lack of response is a hard no from everyone, I tap the tube on my palm to dislodge the paper inside. It comes out easy and there's nothing distinctive about it. I unroll it and scan the words before letting it snap into its rolled form. I'm not surprised when it gives a little shudder and burns up, leaving ash and a faint odour of burnt fibres.

"Well?" Fin asks. She moves to the sofa and tucks herself in beside Griffin. Griffin and Belamey are leisurely drinking their coffees and watching me. I take a second to locate Bradig because he has positioned himself at my feet staring silently up, with his hands on his sword and axe. If I hadn't looked down, one of two things would have happened. I would have either launched him across the room when I swung my foot forward to move, or I would have tripped over him and landed in a heap. Neither would have ended well for me, given his fiery nature.

"It was a list of local locations—"

"Locations for what?" Fin asks.

I shake my head in response. "It didn't say."

Fin whips her whole body toward Griffin so fast that she startles Lord Bradig, who breaks into a round of hysterical hiccups, which we all ignore. "Griffin, you need to tell them what Cian wants. When Cian redirected Griffin here to help, he changed the mission slightly."

Griffin stretches and takes a sip of his coffee. "We're to capture Adria alive and take her to him."

Fin whips herself toward me. "There's a special

Spellbinder prison, Allurist Detention Centre. Did you know that?" She flips her hand up at me dismissively. "Doesn't matter. What matters is how great it's going to be to return the favour and force Adria's life into line like she forced yours."

I glare at Fin without speaking, wishing that Aunt Rune's wart-growing charm had more lure for me. Before I mumble random combinations of words to try cursing Fin, she talks again. "Maybe the locations are suggestions of where to find Adria."

"Why would Tawny want us to find Adria? Belamey told us the crows work for her."

Fin smiles and lifts her eyebrows. She locks eyes with me and raises her voice for the benefit of Belamey, who is behind her on the far end of the sofa. "Well, since we don't know who Belamey's source is or how *she* got the information, it could be incorrect." She pauses. "Or maybe Tawny realized that Adria is a bat shit crazy Bwitch that needs to be contained."

I cut my eyes past Fin toward Belamey. His active effort to hide behind his coffee cup is obvious. I wish I could see Griffin's face because he's staring in Belamey's direction longer than necessary, which leads me to believe that he sees something questionable in Belamey's behaviour as well. Lord Bradig has hiccupped his way so he's standing in front of Belamey. His strange eyes are jumping between Belamey and the rest of us. He's hiccupping so wildly now that he has to be in danger of passing out.

Belamey lowers the coffee and his mouth is visibly moving, like he's trying to work words out past his lips, but there's an exaggerated amount of time before he's successful. "What locations?"

I blink.

"What locations, Kori?" He repeats.

I sigh. "The old mill and the cemetery." I make a spur-of-the-moment decision to keep the third location to myself, at least until I check it out. An ulterior motive drives my decision. Kinsley, also known as Adria, and I have unfinished business. I'm not in a hurry to find any new underground tunnels or secret crypts at the cemetery and although I love the beauty of the crumbling stone walls at the old mill, I don't think the brown, carp-filled water surrounding the arched footings of the walls will be a draw to the talisman. *Chimmi*, I think with an internal eye roll. Besides that, the mill's proximity to the dam just seems too noisy and hectic.

Fin looks confused as she stares at me. "There were only two spots? Kori, two items aren't worthy of being labelled as a list."

I shrug at Fin in response and try to keep my deceit from being readable on my features. Thankfully, everyone is distracted enough by the anticipation of Belamey's response that they overlook me.

Belamey closes his eyes and scratches his neck. He sighs before he opens his eyes. "Those aren't locations for Adria. Those are probable locations for

Chimmi, but in that sense, there is potential to find her too."

Lord Bradig's hiccups stop, and the room is silent as we consider Belamey's words. Lord Bradig looks from Belamey to each one of us. His body is shaking with silent hiccups, which erupt into loud violent bursts on cue with Fin's voice. She bolts up off the sofa, turns to face Belamey, and plants her hands on her hips. "Why would you say that? Is Tawny your secret source? And why, of all the places in the world, would Chimmi come here to Lindsay, Canada?"

Belamey stands with his eyes on Fin. Griffin remains seated, but he stretches his legs out between the two of them to put his feet on the table. Fin and Belamey are both suddenly very charged and I question what Griffin's leg barrier will accomplish if either of them attacks the other. Lord Bradig must have had the same thought because he's positioned himself in front of Belamey with his hands on his weapon's handles.

Fin's voice comes out in a low growl. "If you hurt her . . ." She lets the warning hang, but there's no question of who she's talking about. Belamey's eyes flick to me. Three things happen at lightning speed. Belamey's phone dings, Fin whips a sofa pillow at him, and Lord Bradig shreds the pillow mid-air with his sword, bathing the room in tiny feathers. The feather's light strokes against my skin have a surreal feeling.

From somewhere in the whiteout, Belamey's voice

materializes. "Those locations are full of nature. They'd be comfortable hiding places for Chimmi. If nothing else, this is a starting point. Lord Bradig and I will go to the old mill. You guys head to the cemetery." When the feathers settle, a puff of black smoke lingers where Belamey and Lord Bradig had been standing.

Fin spins on me. "I hate it when he does that, disappearing in a puff of smoke like a magician."

It's impossible not to smile at the look on her face. She looks like a little girl who was just bested by her mean older brother. It doesn't last. Fin can't resist responding with a smile and her face lights up. Her smile lingers for only a second. "I'm sorry, Kori. I don't like how he's acting. He's hiding something from us and I can't stand not knowing what it is. Secrets aren't good, especially when The Squad of Influence requires such trust in order for us to succeed."

"The Squad of Influence?" Griffin asks from his spot on the sofa. He has returned his feet to the floor and looks relaxed.

"Yeah, that's us. All of us, employees of The Recruiter. I figure The Society of the Blood Wind has a cool name, so we need one too."

Griffin is nodding his head throughout Fin's explanation. There's a twinkle of amusement in his eye as he listens to her. "I hope I get to be there when you present that name to Cian."

"Present it to Cian. What, like he makes all the decisions? Like he's the boss . . ." Griffin is chuckling now, and Fin pauses, thinking about what she said. "Okay, so he's the boss, but I think he's making a fundamental management error by not giving us a name to represent us and all we do."

"How do you know there isn't already a name?" he asks her with a smile.

"I . . . Well . . . Listen here Griffin, if there was a name and you didn't share it with me, then the next time we're alone I'm not going to—"

"Hey, hey," Griffin says with his hands up and his smile wide. "I don't know the answer. I was just suggesting that nobody ever asked."

Fin blows out a sigh. "Good, I didn't want to finish that sentence. I don't know what I was thinking. I almost tortured myself to punish you."

Griffin is chuckling as he stands up. I need to decide if I'm going to investigate the third location alone before they suspect me and I lose the opportunity. So, before I think too much about it, I step in behind Fin and slip my arms around her waist. I lean in and kiss her on the cheek. "Can you and Griffin check out the cemetery yourselves? Don't be mad," I say. I push like I'm trying to force my insides out. Although I have been practising Belamey's smoky disappearance magic, it still requires I focus hard to do it successfully. I know that I've succeeded when I feel like the very atoms of my body have separated and become light and airy.

"Shit," Fin says. She's staring at a pale orange-red smoke that's lingering in the space where my body was moments ago. I use the smoky distraction to slip out of the apartment.

Chapter 10

It's colder outside than I expect, and I'm thankful I slipped a pair of toe socks on with my winter sandals. I'm also thankful for the thick sole that's currently keeping the sides of my feet from touching the snowy sidewalk. I hurry west, my goal is to head north on Lindsay Street before Fin and Griffin leave the apartment. The cemetery is south on the same street, and I don't want them to see me.

I'm almost running when I turn the corner onto Lindsay Street. The sound of the dam is like a wall. Without the buildings obscuring it, the rush of water is loud. I make a conscious decision to stay on the west sidewalk until I pass Old Kent Street because Old Kent leads directly to the dam where Belamey and Lord Bradig are exploring. The bridge over the waterway is slippery from the rising mist. The air smells of algae, even in the cold of winter. Over the dam, I can see the crumbling stone wall of the mill, but there's no movement. I breathe a sigh of relief as I cross Lindsay Street and disappear behind the buildings that line King Avenue.

King Avenue is rarely busy, so it isn't surprising that I'm the only person moving. My destination isn't much farther. I stop at the opening of the dead-end street and adjust my toque so it's covering my ears. Shifting my scarf, I move one foot in front of the other, loitering. There are a handful of houses on this dead-end street. In the summer, they become overgrown, offering refuge to some of the seedier individuals that lurk on the streets. As I look now, these houses are so deteriorated they can't be structurally sound, but without wild summer foliage, the houses are the only place to hide.

I refocus toward the end of the street, where the chain-link fence marks the drop of the hill. I hurry forward, eager to climb over it and start my treacherous descent to the train tracks below. Three-quarters of the way down, I pick my way vertically across the hill, using trees to keep me from plunging to the bottom. When I see the aged brick of the abandoned factory, I'm surprised by how it has faded to an ugly pink. Almost none of the brown factory window glass is left; just jagged and deadly pieces. I wince, my childhood memory of this place differs from the reality of it. *A romanticized childhood hideout. It hasn't gotten any safer.*

The temperature has dropped a few degrees, and

my breath is coming out in soft pillows. I strain to hear anything in the silence, but there's nothing to be heard. I grasp the brick of the window frame and hoist myself up. The broken windows illuminate the interior of the factory in patches of light. My footsteps echo loudly in the haunting interior. Rubble from years of vagrancy and rebel teenagers litters the space, from graffiti on the bricks to substances I don't want to think about coating the floors. The winter temperatures have dulled the unpleasant smells that linger here and only a faint earthy smell is present.

I stand and wait for my eyes to adjust to the dimness, preferring not to use artificial lighting. As they adapt, I note that without garbage, this place would be mystical. Even in the winter, without the leaves, the vines and tree branches twist and twine framing the window sills and lacing through holes in the brick, creating an otherworldly feel. If I was a talisman, this is where I'd hide. *Chimmi, why can't I just call it Chimmi?*

I carefully pick my way over the frozen ground, looking for niches where a smaller creature could conceal itself. My magically amplified hearing tips me off, and I mask myself as I dive to the side. The blast hits the wall instead of me. Pieces of branches and bits of brick fill the air. Crouched, I remain invisible, as I peek from my cover behind the stack of wood pallets.

"Come on out, Kori." Her voice inflicts painful feelings like it's raining vinegar, and I'm standing in it with millions of paper cuts covering my body. "I won't throw another orb." In reality, her voice is honeyed, sickeningly sweet and inviting.

Even though I know the voice is Adria's, I can't help widening my eyes when her physically fit 130-pound body steps into view. *Blazing hell!* She looks great in her vintage camo cargoes and form-fitting army coat, tactical and professional. Both of her arms are stretched down toward the ground, palms forward, and glowing with power blast orbs. She lets them blink out. "We should probably talk, Kori. Things didn't end well between us the last time."

I hear the smirk in her voice. I clench my fists. It isn't any easier this time to unclench them than it was the day, almost two years ago, when I found her banging my husband in my home, but at least that day, I got to punch someone. Recalling Carter's naked ass hitting the ground when I laid him out brings a tiny smile to my lips. I unmask myself and step out of my hiding spot.

Adria and I are both silent as we assess each other. She nods thoughtfully. "It wasn't personal then, and it won't be personal now, Kori. For me, it's just a job. A means to an end that I plan to achieve."

My eyebrows have climbed into my hairline. "A job? Screwing my husband and destroying my life isn't personal? Blazing hell, Adria! Is Adria even your name?"

She nods again. "It hurts me too. You and I could have made a killer team. And yum, that Belamey.

Maybe we should share him, too."

My eyes are so wide by this point that I'm sure parts that aren't normally exposed are going to have frostbite.

She shrugs. "I've never been very good at meeting the mothers." Pausing, she watches me for a response. "Well, we better get this over with," she says, like we're about to complete some unpleasant mundane task. Her right hand lifts, and I notice that her pointer finger, from her knuckle to the tip of her manicured nail, has a fancy-patterned ring of silver on it. She pinches her pointer finger and thumb together. There's a chain from the knuckle part of the pointer finger ring to her thumb, which is dressed similarly to the finger. The action causes a stirring to the left of her. And there it is, that mini gorilla face on a hamster's body. Its triangular ears with black tufts of fur on the ends are flattened. Its wide eyes display a terror my words can't describe as its hands, three fingers and two thumbs, cling to a tree branch.

I barely have time to register that there's a small silver item pushed into Chimmi's neck before Adria tackles me. The air rushes out of me when we hit the frozen ground. Adria wastes no time, and her fist smashes into the side of my head. I'm unsure if the impact of it is echoing in my head or the warehouse.

Bucking her hard enough to shift the advantage in my favour, I roll over her like a lioness going in for the kill. The time we spend rolling on the cold ground, punching, kicking, and clawing feels endless. Why it surprises me when she introduces magic to the battle is beyond me. But her orb strikes, lifting and throwing me seven feet off the ground. I slam into the wall, and I hear my ribs crack on impact. Then when I hit the floor, I can't keep the scream in. It tears out of me without conscious thought as something sharp rips through the flesh of my thigh. I coat my body in a protective shield with a charge to deter any physical contact. Unsatisfied, I cuss at myself for surmising based on our history that she would share the desire for a hands-on and magic-off fight. There isn't any point in blinking out of sight because I'm impaled. Instead, I add a dome as an additional level of protection. I try not to focus on the fact that I have no idea how I'm going to live through this. All I can do at this point is fight to remain conscious because if I pass out, the shields won't hold.

"That was fun," Adria says. The blood dripping from her nose is freezing to her skin. Between that and the various other marks our fight left on her face, she looks like she was in a car wreck; not so professional anymore.

She's moving her fancy pointer finger and thumb rings. I take a second to register that Adria's strange rings are controlling Chimmi. It's struggling against her but losing the battle as its arms are forced to detach from the branch that she left it clinging to. Adria continues to motion with her thumb and pointer, but she reverts to me. She swipes at a strand of her raspberry-coloured hair like she's offended it dared to come loose from the messy bun in which she secures it.

Moving closer to me, she crouches, batting her long eyelashes and giving me her eerie, toothy grin. She brings her left hand into view and holds it there, watching my face for recognition. I don't imagine my pained expression can shift much more, but whatever twitch she sees makes her reveal more of her teeth.

I recognize the black orb spinning over her palm. It's strangely beautiful with its wild pulses of white, green, and purple electricity like a lightning storm caught in a ball. Leave it to Adria to present death this way. I have no desire to see death as beautiful, especially my own. But I'm aware of the warm pool of blood forming under me from my leg; when the object drove through my thigh, it likely hit an artery. Losing blood coupled with the pain is sapping my strength. I can barely hold the protective magic I have in place. *Exploding into millions of misty, sparkling particles might not be so bad. Fast and painless.* I immediately hate myself for the thought, and the anger gives me a surge of vigour and resistance. My death orb forms over the palm of my left hand, where it lies on the ground.

Adria opens her mouth with her lips still pulled back, but now her toothy grin has a gap between the top and bottom rows. I can see her tongue flicking across her teeth. "I enjoy your challenge, Kori." Her arm lifts. Before she can throw the orb, a visible wind, the colour of the sky during a summer storm, crashes into her side. The earthy smell of the ground drying after a rainfall fills my nostrils. Adria tumbles sideways in an unnatural somersault until she's out of sight. Her orb dislodges without being aimed and explodes somewhere off to the side.

Despite the cold, I'm sweating. The little beads of moisture are obscuring my vision. I see a small patch of green moving and a flash of glowing orange. *Lord Bradig.* As soon as his name registers, my eyes focus. He's standing by Chimmi. Adria has already recovered, and she's charging toward them. Lord Bradig arches his arm, and releases his axe. In slow motion, I see it spinning end over end toward Adria. Her ringed finger and thumb snap together, and she and Chimmi blink out of sight, but not before Lord Bradig snaps his hand out toward Chimmi. In a sudden sharp movement, its strange-shaped hand grabs something, and then it's gone.

Lord Bradig's hand goes up, and the axe returns to it like a boomerang. My magic fades at that moment. I hear the faint whisper of my voice. "I'm so tired."

There's pain when I wake, but it's distant. I fight panic when I realize I can't move or see. But the panic fades almost as quickly as it surfaced. There's a strange feeling inside my head, like fingers are physically manipulating my brain, massaging it, soothing it, and encouraging it. I notice various sounds of nature, but I realize that I'm not hearing the sounds with my ears. Instead, the sounds are present inside my body, a healing presence. There's a rustle of long grass, like something has disappeared into it and left a soft breeze blowing in its wake, and there's warmth like a blazing sun kissing my body. Then there's silence and no sensation, no pain.

I peek my eyes open to find Lord Bradig crouched low. He leans forward, placing his hands on the ground. I'm briefly reminded of a dog bowed down, wanting to play. But his luminescent eyes are not playful as he studies my face. "Very foolish, Kori, the renowned," he scolds, standing. "You may sit, but not rise yet."

Unsure, remembering my injuries, I creep into a sitting position. I'm not struggling to breathe, and there's no pain when I inhale or exhale. My pants are ruined. There's a large tear in the fabric where the object penetrated, as well as blood in differing stages of freezing covering the front of me. My flesh, visible through the hole, is red and angry, but beyond that, there's no evidence of a wound. "You can heal things, Lord Bradig?"

"No, Kori, the renowned, but I can help the brain

heal things."

The feeling of fingers on my brain and the sensations of nature inside of me take on a new meaning. I look up from my body and blink at him. "Thank you, Lord Bradig."

He starts hiccupping for the first time since I woke up. "It's grand."

"How'd you find me?"

"Belamey, the eminent, sent me to find you. He believed you might not be safe."

"How?" I ask, shaking my head in disbelief.

His hiccups increase to where he can only get one word out. "Source."

His discomfort is evident in his rapid hiccupping. "Do not ask me, Kori, the renowned. I can't have my mouth break my honour."

I restrain my mechanical eye roll. "Very well, Lord Bradig. I'll ask Belamey directly." My voice hitches an octave in the last word of my sentence. I give my body an internal assessment and note that I'm not ready to move yet. "The creature," I blurt out. "I mean, Chimmi?"

Lord Bradig's chubby cheeks puff out more when he smiles. "I will find it. For now, it travels."

I blink my confusion at him. The crunch of feet on the frozen ground on the far side of the building indicates someone is coming.

"I'm knackered, Kori, the renowned. We cannot fight, should we need to."

Although it seems unlikely that it would be Adria

or her people, neither Lord Bradig nor I want to wait to see. I nod my agreement and wobble to standing. My leg feels weak, but I'm well enough to climb out of the building. We decide going down the hill to the tracks and following them farther east to where they feed out of this ravine will be easier than climbing up. I know we'll eventually come to a road where we can get a taxi. As we move away from the building, there are flashes of magic inside.

We watch for a second. "A cleanup crew! She doesn't want evidence of Chimmi to be found."

"She's sleeven, that one." Lord Bradig turns and starts down the hill. "Lord Bradig, what do you call Adria?"

He stops to look at me like I should already know the answer. "She is known as Adria, the ignoble," he says with a hiccup. Then he turns and sets a fast pace east down the tracks.

Chapter 11

Fin takes one look at me when Lord Bradig and I walk in, and I have a definitive conclusion about how bad I appear. Without a word, she inclines her head to him, hooks arms with me and drags me into the bathroom. The steam from the shower clouds the room within seconds. She reaches in and adjusts the temperature before fixing me with an unimpressed facial expression. She puts her hands on her hips. "You have ten minutes to get yourself cleaned up. If you aren't out by then, I'm coming in."

There's no doubt in my mind about her commitment to that phrase. I try to look sheepish. Fin turns and saunters out of the bathroom, closing the door behind her. I hear her laugh from the other side. I flick my hand dismissively, strip down, and climb carefully into the shower. The pooling water is a rusty colour, a mixture of blood and dirt. I wash gingerly. Although Lord Bradig helped to heal my more serious injuries, the soap creates a burning sensation in every scrape and cut it touches. There are more of them than I realized, but that's the price of battle on frozen ground littered with stones, sticks, and garbage. I'm also aware that deep bruises will develop over the next few days. With a sigh, I turn the shower off.

I'm not surprised to find that Fin has taken my destroyed clothing and replaced it with a clean wardrobe of sleepwear. I dress quickly and move toward the smell of coffee.

Fin shoves a mug in my hand and holds her palm up in front of my face to silence me, even though I wasn't planning to speak. I thwack her outstretched hand and wave my coffee under my nose. My eyes slit as I inhale deeply. The heat from my cup warms my nasal passage and fills it with lightly caramelized nutty notes of bitter coffee. My taste buds ache in response.

"Lord Bradig has already informed us about your run-in with Adria. I'm not asking you what you were thinking because I know you enough to know the answer." Fin pauses and attempts to look at me sternly. She fails miserably, with a smirk twitching the corners of her mouth and a mischievous twinkle dancing in her eyes. "We have other things to talk about."

I sip my coffee, enjoying its burnt nutty taste and smell. I slide onto a stool at the breakfast bar.

Tucking my feet under me, I blow on my coffee, and keep my eyes focused on Fin. Griffin is leaning against the counter in his typical pose. Confident and relaxed, with one hand tucked into the pocket of his jeans and the other arm hanging loose at his side. His clear, pale blue eyes watch Fin as she dominates the room with her voice and presence. I'm so busy observing how he watches her that I almost miss what Fin says. I pull my eyes in her direction. "What do you mean, Adria left a message?"

Fin slides a two-inch apothecary vial in front of me on the counter. On first inspection, I note that it's a dirty vial, stoppered with a tiny wine cork. I raise my eyebrows.

"Look closer, Kori."

The bottom of the vial has a dark, tar-like substance covering it. Bits of the strange substance have splattered the inside of the jar. With my face close, I see something inside, moving like a tornado. The dark substance is being pulled into the swirl of air. It's moving so fast that if I wasn't looking with intensity, I wouldn't see it. I cast my eyes at Fin and then down again. I launch away from the jar. Griffin expects my response and keeps me from falling off the stool with hands of air. His throaty chuckling is a welcoming way to ground me. I blink and lean toward the vial.

With the rapid movement inside the jar stopped, the contents become clear. An angry face pushes against the glass, baring a mouth of sharp pointed teeth. The whole creature is half an inch tall. Its face is distinctly human, size, and lack of lips being the only exception. It's hairless, earless, and naked. Behind it, its ragged grey wings open and close with such wilfulness that I'm reminded of a cat's twitching tail when it's angry and getting ready to strike. This enraged creature has two dirty hands pressed to the vial on either side of its head. Its teeth are working against his prison wall as its beady metallic eyes glare at me. None of that concerns me like it should because I focus on the almost impossible-to-read note smashed between its hand and the glass. It reads, "From Adria."

I swallow and blink. "This is Adria's message?"

Fin nods.

"What is it?"

"I swear this is the same bug I squished with your flip-flop in Costa Rica." Fin bends down and peers into the vial. "Curse." She taps the glass softly and the creature turns toward her. We can't hear it, but by the way it holds its mouth, I think it's hissing at her. "There were two in there, but it ate the other one." She stands and moves beside Griffin.

"A curse," I repeat. I look at the vial again. The tornado has returned, and the creature isn't visible as it speeds around in the tiny space. "Nope," I say, trying to move my brain through what I'm seeing and being told. "I don't get it."

Griffin's rough, low voice takes the lead. "There has been limited evidence of their existence, but one hasn't been physically seen in centuries. They're called curses, like the normie term for invoking supernatural power to inflict harm or punishment. This, of course, is not what a normie sees, hears, or believes a curse to be. Normies believe curses to be terrible luck or bad karma. This," Griffin aims a casual nod toward the vial, "is the tangible version. In the Spellbinder world, we don't deceive ourselves about them."

I suck in a deep breath. "Not seen in centuries? Why now?"

"They're rare," Fin says with her eyes straying up and down Griffin's body.

I ignore her and look at Griffin. "What does it do?"

"What they can do varies between them. So, for simplicity, they cause havoc in large numbers, but just a solo one has one of two purposes. It's here to cause bad things to happen or," he pauses, allowing us to contemplate the vial. The curse is gnawing at the glass jar with its weapon-like teeth. "It's deadly."

The room is silent. It takes a marked effort to yank my eyes from the brute, but they just snap back. It's spinning again inside the jar. I'm sure I can hear a faint whirling sound. I feel my head drifting closer to the jar. The curse's grey wings blink in and out of focus in an intentional act. "Open it!" Fin yells. There's a flurry of activity by the counter, but the vial has entranced me. I can see movement in my peripheral vision, and it takes a minute for me to realize that it's my own hands creeping forward.

Without warning, Lord Bradig's long dirty toes flank each side of the vial as he reaches down and snaps it off the counter. My eyes race up his bowed legs and round belly to his wrinkled face. He's holding the vial so close to his mouth that his muzzle is grazing it. He tugs the stopper out, closes his mouth on the open end of the vial, tips his head up and produces a sucking sound. His mouth creates a popping noise when he pulls the vial out. He makes a noticeable swallow, lowers his head down, and hiccups.

I blink. The action is like fog falling away. There's no more activity by the counter because Griffin has Fin in a bear hug. "Blazing hell, what just happened?"

"Kori, the renowned, that sleeven little curse almost made everything go arseways." Lord Bradig hiccups. "He won't get the opportunity to try that again," he says, rubbing circles over his belly.

"I have so many questions. How did you find the curse without it finding you, to how did you catch it, and . . . where did my coffee go?" I say, searching around. "Did I put it down? I can't remember doing that." Reaching overtop of the breakfast bar I grab the pot.

"I need another one, too," Fin says, sliding her mug adjacent to mine. "Does what just occurred mean that this curse was here to make bad things happen?"

Griffin shrugs. "Hard to say."

I'm lost behind my steaming sip when it hits me that two of our three groups had some kind of interaction with Adria. I lower my mug, using the clunky mass to centre me as I study Lord Bradig. When he notices, he bounces with diaphragm spasms. I squint my eyes at him. "Lord Bradig, did you and Belamey find the same kind of message from Adria?"

"Indeed."

"And?"

"Belamey, the eminent, wanted to take it with him, but I ate it."

My eyes are wide, and I can't decide what words to allow out of my mouth. Fin, not bound by hesitancy, speaks first. "Another curse?"

Hic. "I didn't give the sleeven wee thing a chance to play any games. Swallowed him right up, I did." *Hic.*

"It won't harm you, Lord Bradig, to eat those foul things?" Fin asks with genuine worry pasted on her face.

"Fin, the reverent, I am honoured that you worry for Lord Bradig, the superlative." His muzzle has curled up in a smile. "No, the curse will not hurt me to eat. I am not like you or the Spellbinders. I can do many things all of you can't." He walks across the countertop to the teapot and lifts it, pouring the contents directly into his mouth from the spout.

I flick my eyes to Fin.

She winks. "Grass tea."

I look at Lord Bradig. "Lord Bradig, where is

Belamey?"

On cue, the door opens, and Belamey prowls in, sporting his untied boots, black cargoes, and form-fitting black cable-knit sweater. I watch as he takes in the scene. I see the usual threads of magic clinging to him, but I also see the soft weave of an additional thread—he's reading the energy in the room. His eyes land on me. Without a doubt, I'm creating the most energy. My level of irritation is bordering on unhealthy.

Belamey comes toward me and reaches for the coffee Fin is offering him. I watch him take a sip without removing his eyes from me. I'm trying to get my response under control. It's currently a smoulder. I'm also trying to figure out my first words. Before I have time to do either, he speaks. "Firecracker, I understand you might be curious about how I knew to send Lord Bradig to your location."

"Curious?" My blood pressure is rising, and it wouldn't surprise me to see steam coming off the top of my head. "I'm not curious, Belamey. I know where you were. You were with your source, Tawny the crow. But why the secrecy?" I'm struggling not to yell.

Fin's voice is quiet. "Does anyone know how to do that cool thing Grama Pearle does where she places her hand on someone and sends calming magic into their person?"

"If any hand touches me, I'll sever it from its owner," I hiss at Fin from the side of my mouth as I continue working to keep my anger at a simmer and the threat of boiling over at bay. "Belamey?"

He shrugs and sips his coffee. "Tawny is not my source."

My eyes tighten. His nonchalance is infuriating.

"Bloodshed amongst ourselves won't be helpful, Kori," Fin whispers from beside me.

I whip my head in her direction and fix her with narrow eyes. She scrunches her face at me. Cautiously, she reaches her hand toward me and starts trying to smooth my facial features into their regular place. "This isn't good for aging. You need smile lines when you earn the title of a crone, not these . . ."

I swat her hand and turn to Belamey. He has used Fin's distraction to reposition himself beside Griffin. Both of them recline against the counter in their blasé bad-boy manner. As I work to relax my flared nostrils and tight lips my anger locks into a simmer. "Tell us about Tawny, Belamey. It's time."

He shrugs again. "Tawny isn't my source. She provides her intel to my source, who then provides it to me. Tawny knows the information makes it to me, but for her to provide it to me directly wouldn't serve her or me very well, for several reasons."

"And who's your source?"

"Can't say just yet."

My voice hitches. "You can't say?"

He shakes his head no and follows by taking a mouthful of coffee.

I have him fixed in a death stare, wondering why

throwing knives from my eyes isn't a trick in the Spellbinder repertoire of magic.

Fin's voice is excited as she cuts into the conversation. "So Tawny is one of us? Are Mayhem and Blake as well?"

"To the best of my knowledge, no. Before Nekane died, he was encouraging Blake to spend less time with Mayhem and Tawny." Belamey grimaces. "He assigned Kyson to mentor Blake. I can't say how much time they spend together."

"And Mayhem?" Fin asks.

"She's kind of rogue. Nobody can get a fix on her or her loyalties. I don't think even she can."

Fin's smile is wide. "Well, at least we can say Tawny is part of The Squad of Influence."

"The what?" Belamey asks with the corner of his mouth quirked up.

I blow a puff of air out and roll my eyes. My anger has dissipated to irritation, but it's manageable.

"The Squad of Influence." Fin repeats.

Belamey looks from Fin to me and then to Griffin. Griffin gives a throaty chuckle and dips his head toward Fin. Belamey focuses on her.

"Well, The Society of the Blood Wind has a name for their . . . um, organization. I realized someone needed to take on naming our group. So, we are The Squad of Influence." She looks so proud of her declaration.

Belamey's mouth is twitching. "Is this open for discussion?"

Fin's face falls. The unpleasant memories of the Just Flavour versus Just Flavour-s arguments haunt me.

The twitch is no longer pulling the corners of Belamey's mouth. He has let the grin steal across his face. "It's just that it's a mouthful, The Squad of Influence. Who would ever call us that?" He goes silent for a minute and rubs his chin between his thumb and pointer finger. He stops the action fast, like an idea has hit him. "The Influencers."

It might be the first time I've seen Fin speechless. She's staring at Belamey. As much as I'm enjoying this rare moment of dumbfounded Fin, my desire to steer the conversation to more productive things wins out. "Since we can't know your source, does she at least have anything useful to say about what we should do? Adria has Chimmi."

"Kori, the renowned, we do not need Belamey's source for this. Lord Bradig, the superlative, will locate Adria and Chimmi."

I avert my eyes from Belamey. "Lord Bradig?"

"I told you, Kori, the renowned, I will find Chimmi, the tutelary. I gave it a tracker to eat. Adria and Chimmi are moving between locations. When that action stops, I will know where to go."

Chimmi, the tutelary! It has another name? I shake my head. It's so full of questions, I'm indecisive about which one to ask first. I hope that the movement of my head will dislodge one and save me from trying to decide. It doesn't, though. Lord Bradig sees my struggle and looks at Belamey. "Have you not explained it to them, Belamey, the eminent?"

"Sorry, Lord Bradig. I'll tell them now." Belamey gives a little bow to him before looking at me and Griffin. Fin is a lost cause. Her mouth is working, open and closed, but she's struggling with her defeat. "Lord Bradig's people have a bond with a talisman like Chimmi. It was a great number of years ago when that talisman bonded to one of them."

"Not just one of us, Belamey, the eminent. It was my mother's grandmother's grandfather's grandmother's sister's son that the creature bonded. So, a very close relative of mine," Lord Bradig corrects. His tiny self puffs up a bit more with each connection spoken.

"Right? A very close relative to Lord Bradig," Belamey says with a smirk. "The point being, Cian sent Lord Bradig to help us with Chimmi because of that connection. Cian was working on the assumption that Lord Bradig's species and Chimmi would have a deeper connection born and sustained within their magic. It proved to be true if Chimmi has trusted his offering of the tracker."

"Our next move will be based on the location that Lord Bradig reads from the tracker," I say out loud to help myself through the idea. "Can I see the tracker?"

Lord Bradig gives a wild, hiccupping laugh. "See the tracker? Kori, the renowned, you are such a character."

Belamey sees my confusion. "It's a biological thing

for him, not a physical item he can show us."

I'm blinking wildly, almost like a twitch. "I saw him give something to the . . . Chimmi."

Belamey nods, but Lord Bradig speaks. "Very good, Kori, the renowned. I gave Chimmi, the tutelary, a tracker bug. When ingested, it will embed itself in the host and, over time, it becomes one with it. The host will be part of the extensive network formed by Lord Bradig, the superlative, and my people."

I put my fingers over my right eyelid and hold the twitch. "Okay," is the only word that I say.

"The Influencers," Fin mumbles. "That's much better than The Squad of Influence."

Chapter 12

"When all else fails, why not eat? Fin, is that your motto?" I ask. She's spending a tremendous amount of energy setting up a smorgasbord at our kitchen island. She has two candles lit, a stack of napkins and cutlery, along with fancy plates to hold the food she ordered from Just Flavours.

"Listen, Kori, my motto, if I had one, would involve dark stallions, sparkling unicorns, and—"

"Insatiable appetites," Belamey chimes in, having come in the door unheard.

With a look and a smile, Fin cocks her head and considers. "It needs work to pretty it up, but I kind of like having a motto. I should probably get a shirt made." She takes the tray of coffees from Griffin and sets them on the counter. "We could make a game of this motto thing."

"What foods are in the bag?" I ask Belamey to

discourage the direction that Fin's mind is going.

He flashes a sexy smile at me and runs a hand through his short spikey quiff-cut black hair. He follows with a wink. Although I'm dissatisfied with the whole secret source situation, I feel my parts tingle in response to Belamey's flirting. I swallow and blink, which draws a deep, playful laugh from him. One whiff of his intoxicating smell, coupled with the current yearning he just stirred up in me, and I can't promise myself that I'll remain upset with him. I'm using the situation as another excuse to delay addressing my feelings for Belamey because they frighten me. So, I continue to keep my distance and my brain continues to play devil's advocate, whispering alternative options.

I switch side of the breakfast bar and stub my toe. Fin has taken the stool we stand on to reach the top shelves in the kitchen and placed a lace towel over it with a fancy plate. I watch as she sets a to-go cup of grass tea on the stool. On the plate, she arranges various grass food items: grass-stuffed portobello mushrooms, spinach gnocchi with grass seed heads, a bowl of alfalfa, and a wheatgrass smoothie. Lord Bradig is rubbing his hand in circles over his tummy while he watches Fin unload a bag of food onto his specially made table.

"If this is the manner of all human discussions and planning, then Lord Bradig, the superlative, has been missing out."

Fin beams at him. "Lord Bradig, I know you have

an affinity for grasses, but I took some liberties ordering for you. There's even a moss cupcake for dessert. I hope you enjoy everything."

Lord Bradig's wild hiccupping is all the response he gives.

She stands and starts organizing the food for us to eat. "We can grab plates and go sit in the living room. We have a lot to discuss." She cast her eyes to Lord Bradig again. "Has Adria stopped moving locations yet?"

His hiccups are so intense that all he can manage is a head shake. It's hard not to smile as he rubs his tummy, shakes his head, and bounces on the spot from the force of his hiccups. I jerk my hand up toward my nose and pretend to rub it so that I hide my smile.

"Okay," Fin says with finality. She waves her hand over the elaborate food spread. "There are some of our usuals here. Classics, I like that better. Some of our classics are here, soon to be called signatures." Her smile is ear to ear. "These are some new items we're discussing for the menu. Let us know how they taste, honest opinions." She fixes Griffin and then me with a pointed stare. "I . . . I mean Belamey and I . . . want to perfect these new dishes. Bon appétit."

My eyes wander over the food: avocado, strawberry, and goat cheese sandwiches, sharp cheddar, bacon, and sour apple grilled cheese, fig-glazed chicken with brie, and strawberry oatmeal bars with a vanilla glaze. There appear to be two new sandwiches that Fin identifies as a pineapple chicken salad sandwich and a dilly turkey melt. I pick the dilly turkey melt. It looks like a fancy grilled cheese with melted Monterey Jack oozing out of it, along with bacon, pickle, onion, and barbeque sauce. I add an oatmeal bar to my plate and grab a Turkish coffee before heading to the living room.

Griffin, Belamey, Fin, and Lord Bradig are already there. Lord Bradig is standing at the far end of the coffee table. I'm surprised that his plate still has food on it. Belamey and Griffin sit on the sofa with Fin on the floor by Griffin's legs. She leans against the sofa with her feet stretched out under the table.

"Kori, I was just asking about the crows and their relationship," Fin says and takes a bite of her sandwich.

Although there's room on the sofa beside Belamey, I choose to sit on the opposite side of them, cross-legged on a pillow. I eye my plate, unsure where to start.

"There's a fast answer to that, Fin. They aren't siblings. Nekane," I hear a slight edge to Belamey's voice at the mention of his deceased father. "Nekane found them living together on the streets. They were rough and scared. They were keeping each other alive." He sighs. "I don't know any of their stories before they came to live with The Society of the Blood Wind. I'm not sure if anyone does. Whatever happened, all three of them are tight-lipped about it. Anyway, he brought them in and started giving them minor tasks to complete together to make them feel useful and to build trust both ways between them and The Society of the Blood Wind."

"They're pretty new then?" Fin asks with a mouthful of food.

"Only a few years now. Trailing me last year was one of their first bigger missions. Everything else you already know." Belamey takes a big bite of his sandwich.

"Well, not everything." Fin corrects. "You must know more about Tawny . . ." She lets the implications hang, hoping Belamey will give more information about his source in relation to Tawny. He just goes on chewing. "Whoever your source is, she clearly has something against The Society of the Blood Wind, an axe to grind or a debt to resolve." Fin looks toward the ceiling, and I can see her mind is working through options.

I see my window to steer the conversation, and I take it. "I think we need to talk about the current problem. Adria and," I pause, "Chimmi."

"Old news, Kori." Fin flicks her hand at me. She rushes on without giving me a chance to raise an eyebrow. "Old news. Adria wants Chimmi because of the power it would give her. Imagine her as the head of The Society of the Blood Wind? She's like Dolion or Nekane with a vagina. With Chimmi bonded to her, her protection from attacks will be infinite. She'll be able to use Chimmi to see paths to the future, and it'll teach her magic that other Spellbinders likely don't know and won't know how to counter. Adria may not want to annihilate the human species, but she isn't seeking Chimmi's power because she wants to make the world a better place. The bitch is evil."

Belamey and Griffin have nothing to add. They just go on chewing and giving an occasional nod of agreement.

"Kori, the renowned, when a creature like Chimmi, the tutelary, came to my people, it was with them for a short time. This species' lives are not long. But many of the powers it imparted stayed, and hints of those powers have travelled through generations. Some powers weakened, others grew, and a few have disappeared, all dependent on how the person practices and grows that power to full strength. The powers that have died out are gone completely."

"Lord Bradig, are you saying that once Chimmi bonds to Adria, she can grow an army through her family line by imparting her views, teachings, and new magic to her offspring and so on down the line?" Fin asks.

Lord Bradig nods and downs his grass tea.

"Holy shit!" Fin says, banging her empty plate down on the table. She looks at each of us with a satisfied look on her face. "I just put it all together. Adria, as Kingsley, used Carter to get sperm and cursed his penis so he couldn't make a baby with you. Not that you would sleep with him after the affair, but why take chances? She disappeared with his sperm, froze it somewhere. She wasn't getting pregnant banging him, she must have collected some to keep trying. Now, once she forces Chimmi to bond to her, she will use the sperm and start her army."

My eyes are explosively wide. "What in the blazing hell are you talking about?"

"It makes sense in an off-handed way," Belamey offers. "She never wanted to be just a part of The Society of the Blood Wind. But being its head, well, that's something else entirely. As for the sperm, the Ember family has always been one of the most powerful Spellbinder families. Maybe not every generation is powerful. Regardless, they have been the strongest force acting against The Society of the Blood Wind. If you were planning a hostile takeover, why not let the two opposing forces help you without knowing they are doing it? In addition, any extra . . ." Belamey struggles for a word.

Fin picks up his thread of conversation. "Any extra drama, however big or small, that she could set against them benefits her as a distraction or a full-out obstacle. It's brilliant. Nobody would ever see her coming."

I'm shaking my head. "Why Carter? Why me?"

Fin hurries into her explanation. "Think about it. Why you? First, she clearly hates you. It's personal, I would say. Second, the only thing better than screwing with Carter," Fin flushes. "Pardon the pun. But Alivia has kids. Adria couldn't cause any waves or scandal there. The only thing better than the scandal she created, destroying your life, would be getting pregnant with Ember family sperm. Imagine her having a baby with genetics from a prominent Spellbinder family. Since your brother, Jaxton, is deceased and the rest of the living sperm carriers in your family are just too old to be of use, she settled for Carter and the scandal."

I'm not buying any of this because I hate being at the centre of things. I know there isn't any value in arguing, but I can't resist pushing at it a bit. "There's a flaw in your theory, Fin. Adria wouldn't have known that Chimmi was going to appear. She likely didn't know about Chimmi at all until someone recently whispered about its existence in the Spellbinder community."

I can't figure out why my statement has Fin smiling. "No, silly, I agree she was ignorant about Chimmi. That doesn't matter. Her initial plan was to weaken the defences of her two biggest problems: your family and the powerful leaders of The Society of the Blood Wind. Chimmi's appearance is a recent addition to her plan."

Lord Bradig blinks into sight in the middle of the table between Fin and I, ending the conversation. "Excuse me, Fin, the reverent, but it is time for us to go. Adria has stopped moving."

Chapter 13

If the last year taught us anything, it's that we can move like a team when the situation requires it. This is one of those times. As soon as Lord Bradig discloses Adria's location, we're up and moving without discussion. I down my coffee, shift, and soar out the window after Belamey. His tail feathers with the three greyish bands are a familiar sight for me, and I trail him with ease. Fin typically follows us in the Bronco. Given that Griffin and Lord Bradig aren't part of our normal team, I assume they'll travel with Fin. Griffin's bird is a black-bearded vulture, so he could fly, but having a Spellbinder with Fin makes sense, especially since we're going after Adria.

Our flight takes us outside town to an abandoned business just off the highway. We circle in the sky, but nothing is moving, and there are no signs that it's warded. Belamey and I land close to the dingy brick building, shift, and arm ourselves with orbs. Overgrown grass pops through the snow, and the yard is full of rusted vehicles. Fin, driving the Willys MB, pulls into the rutted, semi-circle driveway. It's more dirt than gravel, with patches of dry, dead grass throughout. I'm concerned because she just drove in and straight up to the building. She's usually tactical.

My eyes flare when she jumps out and yells at us. She's waving us toward her and making herself a visible target for Adria and whoever else might be inside. Griffin and Lord Bradig are standing beside her and aren't the least bit concerned. I look twice at Belamey when his orbs vanish, and he prowls his way toward them. I rock on my feet with my eyes sweeping the building, assessing for risk, before I follow his lead.

"She's gone," Fin says.

I tense in response but keep my eyes roaming the premises because I don't want to believe that we missed her.

"I figured she was gone when you started waving yourself like a human-shaped car lot balloon that bends and blows in the wind," Belamey says, eliciting a chuckle from Griffin and a kiss-my-ass look from Fin.

"Lord Bradig said she left about five minutes after we got in the car. We had no way of communicating with you. We should have special bird-sized ear pieces made so we can communicate when you fly and I drive." The thoughts are shifting behind her eyes.

Before she can launch herself into the familiar argument about shrinking her to carrying size, I move toward the front door. A wooden patio used to be here. I've never been inside this building, but I remember it. I remember watching the patio gradually degrade and collapse. Another business tried its hand at using this property, so they tore the patio off and poured concrete steps. Looking at the crumbling stairs suggests that someone worked them over to deter people from going inside.

"Anyone see any wards?" I ask over my shoulder. I push out feelers of magic and use them to gain access through the damaged door frame. Nothing comes back to me with any red flags, so I pull the door to open it. It's stuck. I heave, and the door gives way, coming off the hinges completely. I stagger under the unexpected weight of it, unsure how I can correct my balance without falling down the stairs. Then the heat of Belamey's body is pressed against me. He catches the door, and he throws it sideways off the porch.

"Thanks." I see a twinkle dancing in his eye as he nods recognition. My mouth goes dry, my thoughts straying to the personal ways I could make the light in those eyes glimmer. I move before my imagination gets carried away.

Snapping my hands down, slightly angled from my body with my palms forward, I allow sound vibration orbs to materialize in my grip. Knowing Belamey is behind me, I move left through the door and he tracks right.

Expecting a similar setting to the one in the old factory where Chimmi was hiding, the space we enter doesn't disappoint. It's two rooms in a single-storey building with no basement. There's the main front area, which we entered first, and a smaller section attached. The rear section is locked. I have to give the door three kicks to bust it open. The jam by the lock breaks, but this door stays on sturdy hinges as it swings in. We sweep into the room to clear it. This room is a stark contrast to the front. It's also empty of life forms, but it's pristine and freshly renovated. A sweet candy-like bouquet of sour cherry and fresh jasmine hangs in the air. I let my orbs dissipate, disappointed that I didn't get to see them momentarily offset gravity.

Fin enters the room, rolling one of her knives' handles between her palms. "It stinks like Kinsley, I mean Adria. She's been living here! Look at this place."

The room is six feet wide and sixteen feet long. There's a kitchenette with high-end mini stainless steel appliances in one corner, and an open bathroom at the opposite end of the room, with a living and sleeping space in the middle.

"Look at the unique pattern in each floor tile, and this is quartz," Fin says, tapping her knife on the dark grey countertops. "The Bwitch likes grey. She . . ."

I flick my eyes to Fin, wondering why she stopped

her soliloquy. She's peering into the mini kitchen sink drain. "What are you doing?" I ask, moving over to the sink.

She turns the water on full blast. "I thought I saw a curse." She shakes her head as I take a step back. "Couldn't have been, right?"

"Belamey, the eminent, I have found evidence that Chimmi, the tutelary, was here."

We all move toward Lord Bradig. Based on this small area, Adria is treating Chimmi as if it's a hamster. Lord Bradig is bent over, picking something up. When he turns to face us, he's holding up one triangular piece of skin with a tuft of black fur coming out of the tip.

I feel bile rise in my throat. "Is that Chimmi's ear?"

"Kori, the renowned, Chimmi, the tutelary, is moulting in its efforts to resist Adria, the ignoble, and her . . ." Lord Bradig is tapping two of his fingers together in an open-and-closed motion. I blink at him. "Kori, the renowned," he says, still tapping his fingers. "The item Adria, the ignoble, was using to control Chimmi, the tutelary?"

I realize he's waiting for me to give it a name. I was showering when Lord Bradig told Fin and Griffin what happened at the factory. So, I don't know if he told them about the device. "It was a ring." Based on the looks on their faces, they knew Adria had captured Chimmi, but they didn't know any further details. Knowing of Chimmi's imprisonment seems like enough knowledge at the outset. Knuckling my fingers into the back right side of my neck I provide the answer. "It isn't a typical ring. It covered her full pointer finger, and a chain attached it to a similar ring on her thumb. There was a silver object in Chimmi's neck. Movement of the ringed thumb and finger controlled Chimmi."

"She's leashed it, and it's having predator-induced stress." Fin crinkles her nose. "And social living stress."

Lord Bradig is hiccupping, his animated endorsement.

"Knowing it's resisting is something, but how long can it do that for?"

"Lord Bradig," Fin says. Her voice has a note of dread in it. "Are we looking at a situation where Chimmi can resist 'til its death or bond and live?"

He's hiccupping too much to answer.

"It's unknown, Fin." Belamey's husky voice provides a reply I refuse to spend time thinking about. "We can presume, based on Spellbinder and normie history. We see patterns that suggest exerting the right amount of force, in the right place, for long enough . . ." Belamey's sentence and the silence hang heavy in the air.

The chill that runs up my spine, as a result, breaks me from the spell. "There isn't anything else here to help us," I say. "Lord Bradig, do you know where Adria and Chimmi went?"

"What the connection allows me to see is vague and obstructed, Kori, the renowned."

"Wait," Fin says. "Can the tracker be removed?"

Lord Bradig's hiccups have dwindled enough that he can form words again. "Not without death, Fin, the reverent. It's growing inside Chimmi, the tutelary, and not yet at full strength, but it cannot be removed."

"Adria wouldn't be able to detect it, would she?" I ask. "And she didn't see you pass it to Chimmi."

"That is correct, Kori, the renowned."

"It seems unlikely that she plans to come back here, and even if she did, she wouldn't stay in a compromised hiding place." I sigh. "Lord Bradig, can you describe anything from the hazy vision that might help us determine where she is?"

"Do we need to do this here?" Fin asks.

"I see." Lord Bradig closes his orange eyes and snaps them open again with a string of hiccups. "Tunnels. She went underground."

"Given what we learned about your parent's house last year, Kori, that isn't helpful information because she could be anywhere. We don't know what kind of network runs under this town. And blocked and hazy sounds warded to me," Fin says.

Belamey curses under his breath. He has a look of extreme discomfort.

"Is it time, Belamey, the eminent?"

"Yes, it is." Belamey scowls.

Fin is vibrating with excitement. "Time for what?"

"It's time to meet my source. She's staying with Talon," he says grudgingly. Talon and Belamey's strange behaviours when we were at the safe house suddenly make sense. I blow out a long sigh and try to ignore my aching body.

Fin slaps her hands together and rubs them. "This is the best day! There has been sex, a glowing penis, a message from Tawny, a confrontation with Adria, the discovery of curses, uncovering Adria's hideout, and soon we meet Belamey's source."

Belamey shifts. A blurred description of man and bird, fill my mind as I watch: large, powerful, and impressive. Dark-grey-feathered wingbeats propel Belamey, the harpy eagle, from the building to dominate the sky. I feel a primitive biological hunger. If Fin could hear my thoughts, she'd say, "Animal magnetism."

Chapter 14

I'm trying to keep my mind distracted by focusing on the number of trees racing by between neighbouring properties. So many trees hide the safe house driveway that I'm unsure how we don't drive by. Fin waves at Daken and Galox when we drive past the front door. No matter how many times I observe those sleek, cement-looking gargoyles, I'm always apprehensive when they move. Today is no different. Their muscular bodies stand facing the trees that line the main roadway. Daken turns toward the Willys as we drive by, and I get a good look at his compact, deep-chested body. Behind him, the barbed end of Galox's spiked tail is twitching as she pretends to ignore our arrival.

"This is going to be great," Fin says, as she parks. "I can't wait to meet Belamey's mysterious source."

Talon stands in silence, watching us approach.

His face is obscured by the hood of his grey robe, but his presence on the porch is a sign that Belamey arrived before us and explained the situation. Talon says nothing. He turns toward the sunroom door and opens it. The birds in the sunroom are quiet. It creates a feeling of apprehension when barely a chirp comes from the room, even after we enter.

"Talon?" I say.

He stops at the threshold to the kitchen, pivots, and removes his hood. His big round eyes look as surprised as ever. His head is bobbing. "Coffee should be ready for us. We'll convene in the kitchen." He turns and hops through the doorway.

Fin shoves me like she's going to break into a sprint. By reflex, my eyes roll. I move over to let Griffin and Lord Bradig go past. I suck a deep calming breath of air and try to prepare myself for whatever is about to come next.

Fin's voice echoes into the sunroom. "Holy shit!"

I round the corner into the kitchen to find Fin pumping the arm of a short, slight woman who looks too young to be Belamey's mother. But with her cinnamon hair and sun-kissed skin, it's impossible to mistake her for anyone else. *Missing since Belamey was three? All the sacrifices she made, can it really be Rye Juniper-Adelgrief? Missing and not dead.* The same intensity that radiates off Belamey is emanating from her. She fixes on me with pale brown eyes. I freeze, unsure of what to do or say.

The woman crosses the kitchen and wraps me in

a motherly embrace, firm and warm. My unease is gone, replaced by a feeling of familiarity that's confusing but welcome. "I've been dying to meet you, Kori. Sorry for the secrecy," she says, releasing our hug and shooting a stern look at Belamey, who shrugs and looks amused. "My apologies, as well, for monopolizing Belamey's time. As you can imagine, after years of apparent absence, he and I have a lot of catching up to do." I know my face twitches as I work through what's happening. The woman takes my hand in hers and leads me toward the table. "I'm Rye Juniper, Belamey's mother."

My mind is racing. "It's a pleasure to meet you, Miss Juni—"

"It's Rye, dear. You can call me Rye or mother. It would hardly be appropriate for Belamey's fiancée to call me anything but."

If my eyes could explode out of their sockets, this would be the time. Before I can respond, Fin slams a coffee mug down on the table, spraying me with drops of coffee and soaking the table with a large slosh. She dives at my left hand and rockets it up into her face, searching my finger for any sign of a ring. She drops my hand with a tut and gives a scolding look at me and then at Belamey.

"Coffee, Rye?" Fin asks, all business-as-usual.

"Yes, please, dear."

Fin slips a mug of coffee in front of Rye and slides into a seat that affords her a good view of Rye and me. "So, you aren't dead, Rye," Fin says casually.

Rye gives a pleasant laugh. "It would appear not."

"Wow." Fin's head is bobbing up and down. "One mystery solved. You've been missing, not dead." Fin flashes a huge smile at me. My lips are compressed and I'm pinching the bridge of my nose with enough pressure that it might bruise, which entices Fin's smile lines to deepen. "Don't worry, Kori. We'll return to the whole fiancée thing, but first, I need to know more about Rye's missing person persona."

I'm working so hard not to look at Belamey that I have neck and eye pain. *Belamey's fiancée? Smoke and ashes!* I don't have a chance to follow that train of thought down the spiral.

"Not missing, either, if you know where to look," Rye corrects. Fin is blabbering away and Rye uses it as a cover for her next remark. "Kori, deciphering visions is open to the interpreter." A look passes between Rye and Belamey that implies this comment is to ease the panic she reads in my features.

"I'm excited to hear your escape plan, how it played out, who helped you, where you've been, and how long has Belamey known?" Fin looks to Belamey. "I'm hurt that you, my business partner, left me in the dark about this."

Belamey opens his mouth to respond, but Rye cuts in. "I'm sure you have lots of questions, dear. We all do. Satisfy yourself with the obvious details."

Fin can't help herself. "Does Grama Pearle know you're here?"

Rye is silent. She shifts her whole body in her chair

so that she's completely facing Fin. Whatever Fin sees in Rye's expression makes her swallow and look abashed. I'm so surprised by it that I fight the urge to jump up to see Rye myself. Rye's voice comes out soft but pained. "Pearle doesn't know yet, Fin. That will be a hard reunion for both of us, especially now that Birdie is gone." Rye shares a brief sad smile with Talon. "Kori's mother, Cora, is also unaware."

"I'm sorry, Rye," Fin responds with her eyes still down.

Rye pales and looks tired. "Me too, dear. I'm also sorry, but the rest of this discussion will have to wait until the morning." She stands, takes Fin's hand into her own, and pats it. She moves to Belamey and hugs him. His arms envelop her, and his eyes close as they hug. "Goodnight, my dears," Rye says as she glides from the room. Belamey's head is dipped, and he watches from hooded eyes.

My night's sleep was short but restful. Now we're all sitting at the kitchen table with two full pots of fresh coffee. Fin and Belamey prepared French toast roll-ups filled with a delicious apple pie filling. The smell of cooked apples and cinnamon mixed with the coffee is intoxicating. I plop that first bite into my mouth and chew, savouring the burst of flavour on my tongue. The texture is cakey, and sticky, with a crunch. I swallow and lift my coffee to my lips, eyes closed, and chase my food down with a hot sip.

After a respectful number of mouthfuls, Rye restarts the conversation that we left unfinished last night. "Now, it's my understanding that we have a hazy vision and underground tunnels to discuss. Lord Bradig, if you've finished your grass tea, would you care to tell me what you see through your connection with Chimmi?"

I'm surprised, but this time it's regarding how much Rye knows, given how well she's hidden for the last thirty-one years. I wonder how long Belamey has known that his mother isn't dead. Nothing in his face or posture implies that this is a surprise reunion.

Lord Bradig's hiccups are his trademark and something has excited him. My mug is frozen mid-sip, my focus on him.

"Dark tunnels and dim light." A hiccup punctuates each word. "Some walls are crumbling, but other walls look well kept."

Rye's compressed facial features and raised hand with her finger pressed sideways against her lips suggests this means something to her. "Lord Bradig, can you see if there's anything unique in the space: symbols, statues, any kind of ornamentation?"

Lord Bradig gives a string of violent hiccups, closes his eyes, and falls silent. His body convulses, but no sound escapes. Minutes pass. I empty my mug and look longingly at the bottom, wishing I could magically refill it. It's unclear what makes me look up when I do, but I witness Lord Bradig's luminescent eyes fly open. A group of hiccups burst out of him so violently that they throw him off his feet. He blinks out of sight before we see him hit the ground. He can't block the sound of it, though. "That went arseways fast," he grumbles.

"Well, that was new," Fin whispers.

When he reappears, he's standing on the kitchen table in front of Rye. With a smile on her face, she's looking at the exact spot he's in, even before he's visible. "What did you see, Lord Bradig?"

"A strange picture."

"Can you tell me what it looked like?"

"I can do better," he says, looking proud. He rolls his hands like he's cupping a sphere, then he throws them upward, releasing the non-existent ball. In the air over his head, a black and grey image forms. Two long, sideways flames flank a bunch of faded black swirls.

"She's under Dolion's house," Rye breathes.

"Say what?" Fin's response comes out so fast it sounds like a strange noise instead of two words formed into a question. "Dolion, as in The Society of the Blood Wind Dolion? How do you know by looking at swirls in the air?"

"It isn't a bunch of swirls. These are representations of hands, society hands, with a long reach," Rye explains, pointing to what I thought were sideways flames. "The hands hold and release the wind." She's thoughtful for a moment. "Typically, the image is in red."

Fin's head tilts. "They are hands. Wow! The Society of the Blood Wind has an ancient symbol. Cool piece of history, but how are you sure of the image's location?" Fin casts a lidded peek at me, Belamey, and Griffin. She mumbles as she works through her thoughts. "The Influencers need a symbol too. Mental note to me: make this happen." She sighs like she has the weight of a thousand tasks on her shoulders.

Rye nods encouragingly at Fin's symbol commitment. "Because I painted it there. I wanted to mark the room as a Society of the Blood Wind space in case anyone should stumble into it, but I also wanted to make sure I could identify it from the Society should I need to, hence the colour change." Rye takes a turn, looking at each of us. I'm blinking like a fool when her gaze lands on me. She pats my leg gently. "Nekane and Dolion wouldn't use the tunnels. They felt too high and important for such dark and dirty places. They had their own set of modern, sophisticated tunnels built under the house, more like secret walkways in and out. I, however, became intimately acquainted with the older tunnels, the ones they hadn't sealed and warded. They did ward the tunnel entrance into the house, but that's easy enough for me to get through without setting it off. But, what isn't known, I discovered tunnels and rooms long ago forgotten, their entrances concealed from the eye. I imagine there are other tunnels to be discovered. Anyway, I took pains to ensure they remained concealed and accessible only to a few select people. I marked that room with the symbol as a landing point for myself when I returned to the house to visit, unknown to the majority inside." She sighs. "It would seem that someone else discovered it."

"You didn't ward the tunnels or the room?" Fin asks.

"There was no need. My generation was the last to have knowledge about the tunnel's existence. Dolion believes, or at least he used to, that the tunnel system under the house is unusable. Everyone besides me used the fancy new tunnels because those are direct, and you don't need any special knowledge to navigate them. The old tunnels are like an underground labyrinth, and those that I found are the worst. There's one direct entrance to that series of tunnels, but in theory, a person could enter the tunnels from Pearle's store, for example, and eventually find their way to where Adria is. It's complex and can be an unbelievably long time underground, but if the tunnels haven't collapsed or been magically blocked, it isn't impossible."

"Adria has put herself in a perfect position for her surprise takeover of The Society of the Blood Wind if she can force Chimmi to bond with her," I point out.

Fin gets up abruptly and returns with the coffee pot to refill mugs. I had been so busy listening to Rye that I hadn't noticed Talon make a new pot. I also hadn't noticed Lord Bradig plunk his butt down on the table. He's sitting facing Rye with his legs straight out and spread. His green shirt hangs between his legs, concealing things I don't need to get an eye full of. I scrunch my face when he wiggles his butt like he has an itch on one of his butt cheeks. He's grinding his bare ass on the surface of the dinner table.

Fin is standing beside me, pouring a generous amount of coffee into my mug while she reviews our situation. "So, we need in. But we don't know what safety nets Adria has set in place, nor do we know how to get there."

Rye has a twinkle in her eye. "Her safety precautions shouldn't be a problem. I doubt she knows the way into the room that I have in mind for you guys."

"You aren't coming? I assumed that's why we're here," I blurt out, whipping my head in Belamey's direction.

He watches me with the same twinkle in his eye that Rye has. He's relaxed leaning against the wall, one untied boot crossed over the other at the ankle, toned arms laced across his chest.

"You know the tunnel system, Belamey?" Fin cuts in, in her attempt to decipher the twinkle.

He shakes his head no without taking his eyes off of me.

Fin stands at the head of the table with the coffee pot in one hand and her other hand on her hip. "I don't get it. If you aren't coming," she says to Rye. "And you don't know the tunnels," she says to Belamey. Her eyes are flitting between them. "Are we just going to knock on the front door and explain that there's a crazy bitch beneath the basement of the house trying to force a powerful talisman into her control so she can overthrow them and take over the world? I don't think that will work."

Amused, Rye answers. "No. You'll go into the tunnels, Fin."

Fin's mouth drops open and hangs on one word. "Tawny."

Chapter 15

I notice the kitchen window is open, but I don't give it any thought. The room is warm and full of the sweet smell of baking cookies. So, the frosty air from the window offers a delicate balance to the oven heat. The cawing crow perching in the window sill gives the open window a new meaning. Its small round head cocks, and its beady black eyes watch us. The crow hops onto the countertop and shifts, leaving Tawny sitting there with her legs crossed. Her middle finger, the one with the silver tree ring, is up and facing the room. Tawny tips her head to the side. She has a very stereotypical teenage expression of disinterest on her face. It's an improvement to her resting face, best described like she's permanently smelling foulness. Tawny turns her hand, with her middle finger up, and gives us a little wave with it. Rye sees none of this, having never turned from the table.

Tawny slides off the counter. Her high-top black boots make a loud thump as they hit the floor. She smirks and crosses the room in a couple of strides, bends, and puts her arms around Rye. "Hello, Mother Rye." Tawny casts a look at Belamey to see if her use of the title mother will get a reaction out of him. Belamey winks at her. Her cheeks colour. She makes a dramatic flourish, removing her long, hooded black cape. She has deepened the purple of her hair to almost black and magically enhanced its length so that bangs frame her face and a messy loose bun hangs at the nape of her neck.

"I love this look," Fin says, swiping her hand in the air down the length of Tawny. "Black pantyhose under those cute little black shorts, the boots, and that tight turtle neck. Imagine it with a tank top or t-shirt."

Tawny raises an eyebrow at Fin and glances toward the window. Soft snow is falling. "Winter wear, Fin. T-shirts and tanks are spring, summer, and fall." With the sassiness dripping off her words, I'm surprised she doesn't roll her eyes.

"Tawny, I have been aching to ask. Where did you get your ring?"

Tawny smirks and gives Fin the finger. "This one?"

"Yes, that one. First, though, is that sparkle, espresso nail polish?"

"You bet." Tawny reaches into the cape she draped over the chair and flings the polish at Fin. "Try it. Accentuate those long fingers."

Fin splays her hand out and assesses it. "You're right. I totally should." She opens the polish. "The ring, Tawny?"

"It looked like him." Tawny points to Lord Bradig. "Sorry," she says, like one of us called her out on her poor manners. "A creature that looks like Lord Bradig gifted me the ring."

The room has fallen silent as we freeze with her admission. The timer from the oven screams in the silent room. Talon hurries over and returns with a plate of hot chocolate chip cookies.

Tawny snakes a cookie, bites it, chews lazily, then swallows. "Just kidding. Is there milk?" Popping the rest of the cookie into her mouth, she gets herself a glass of cold milk and leans against the counter, facing us, drinking it. She sets it in the sink and comes to the table. Sitting beside Fin, she puts her feet up on an empty chair.

"That's enough theatrics, dear," Rye says.

Tawny gives a slight shrug. "I've always had the ring. I wore it on a necklace until it fit on a finger." She looks at us, her eyes staying on Rye. She twists the ring on her finger, and there's discomfort in her voice when she talks next. "I don't remember my childhood or my family. So, I can't say where the ring came from."

Rye reaches across Fin to place her hand on Tawny.

Tawny's lips twitch at the corners like she wants to smile but can't. "I've always felt the ring and me shouldn't be segregated. I'd say I feel anxious without it, but I can't because it's always with me."

My awareness of a cool feeling swiping over my fingernails is slow. I sigh and tilt my head upward when I feel it. I don't know when Fin started applying the nail polish to my fingers, but she's too far into the process for me to pull my hand away. Fin's head is low to the table where she's painting. "This way, you can't eat the cookies because your nails are wet," she whispers and winks.

I stifle my sigh and do my best to ignore her. I lower my voice. "Tawny, what's your earliest memory?"

"I remember Blake and Mayhem cuddled together and crying. Blake was four. He was so small and scared." She stops moving the ring and holds it between the middle knuckle and the top of her finger. "Mayhem was six. She was fierce when I approached them, like a rabid animal, ready to protect its young." Tawny lowers her hands. "My earliest memories are of my time with Blake and Mayhem."

"And you had the ring, then?" I lift my eyes from her ring, to her face. "Sorry to ask, Tawny. I can't imagine how these memories feel."

She nods and stops fiddling with her ring. Rye seizes the opportunity to steer the conversation. "We should return to discussing the tunnels."

Tawny bolts upright in her chair and leans forward. "I love the tunnels."

"You love the tunnels?" Fin asks.

Tawny nods enthusiastically.

"Aren't they dark, cool, dingy, and empty of life forms?"

"Not all life forms. There are spiders, rats, bats, and a few other—"

"Stop! Just stop!" Fin interrupts. "Let's talk about our mission."

"Wait," I cut in. "Tawny, how did you start working for Adria?"

"Oh, I don't work for her."

"But you knew those locations. How?" I push.

Tawny is spinning her ring again. "Sometimes it knows things." She shrugs. "It's another thing I have no answer to, and I have no reason to question it."

Belamey readjusts his position on the wall. He made up the idea of Tawny working for Adria because how else could he explain without giving away Rye's existence? Fin has recuperated enough from the threat of creepy crawling and flying life forms. "Your ring knows secrets, and it shares them with you?"

Rye laughs and pats Fin on the shoulder. She directs her words to Tawny. "Adria is under The Society of the Blood Wind house. We need to get to her without her knowing we're coming."

With Tawny's constant something-smells expression, it's impossible to decipher what she's thinking. "She's under the house? Does she have Chimmi with her?"

I jerk in surprise. "How much does she know?" I slit my eyes at Belamey and hiss. "She's a fifteen-year-old girl who lives with The Society of the Blood Wind. A house that offered her and her friends refuge from life on the streets."

Tawny's chair screeches as she bounds to her feet. I turn to her, and she's giving me the finger with both hands. "Sorry, Mother Rye." She shifts and sails out the still-open kitchen window.

"That went well," Fin interjects. "Kori, did you even consider that the ring might be the reason Tawny knows so much?" She mumbles under her breath.

Rye stands up and leaves the room without a word. Everyone else is staring at me. I roll my eyes. "What?" I look from face to face. "She's an emotional teenager. Impressionable and living with the enemy. I don't understand why she's trusted with information. How can we be sure of her loyalty?"

"I assume the answer is if Rye trusts her, then the rest of us can," Fin says to me and then shifts her eyes to Belamey, raising her eyebrows. Belamey gives a silent nod. We trust Rye because of her sacrifices and her commitment, a trust earned decades before our lives started. Talon startles me when he hoots, stands, hops, and hurries into the sunroom.

Rye returns to the kitchen. She's carrying a rectangular wooden box mounted on a strap. The box is on hinges, and she flips the clasp open and lifts the lid. It's an artist's box with several elastic holders for supplies. There's a wooden ruler beside the pencils, an eraser, and a few other things, but it's a five-by-seven leather journal that Rye lifts out. The journal's leather is well worn, and a finger-thick twine of aged rope holds the leather cover around the dark, rough edges of the paper. She sets it down and unwraps the twine. The paper's face is a soft brown with a faint pattern.

"Is that cotton paper?" Fin asks.

Rye nods and flips a few pages for us to see. The pages are marked with drawings but minimal words.

I draw my fingers over the soft, smooth paper. "It's maps."

"Yes, and important notes," Rye says with a smile. "I was mapping out the tunnel systems for years. A passion of mine that I had to abandon until recently. Tawny has been helping me complete the project. She shares my love for the tunnels and the secrets they hold. She explores and makes notes and rough sketches, which she brings to me. I transcribe them here."

Talon shrieks in the sunroom. There's a flurry of wings and bird screeches, followed by a loud bang. I bolt toward the sunroom with Belamey on my heels. I skid to a stop when I see Talon's surprised-looking face fixed on me. His hand is pressed against an upside-down glass on the tabletop while his other hand gently shoos birds. The glass contains a tiny spinning tornado.

"Blazing ashes! Is that a curse?"

"A what?" Rye asks.

Lord Bradig blinks into sight beside the glass. He looks at Talon. "Talon, the keeper, please lift your hand."

Talon gives a little hop to disassociate with what's happening. And in a flash, Lord Bradig is on his stomach. He tips the glass sideways, creating a small opening between the table and the rim. His tongue flashes out, frog-like, and disappears into his mouth, taking the curse with it. He stands, gives a loud burp, and hiccups.

"Oh, my," Talon says. "I hadn't been expecting you to do that, Lord Bradig. I kept the birds from eating it so I could study it." He looks comical as his big, round eyes gawk at us. His mouth is opening and closing like a baby bird waiting to be fed a worm.

"Things might be worse than we imagined," Rye says from the back of the group. "Talon, can you tell me what you noticed? Was it truly a curse?"

Talon's head bobs in response, even though Rye can't see him. One question settled, we shift to the kitchen. I bring my fresh cup of hot coffee to my lips when a commotion on the counter makes me jump. The hot liquid sloshes against my face, making me jump again. Tawny has returned, and she's using her middle fingers as flags while smirking at my mishap. I swipe my arm over my face. "Could someone please close that window?"

Tawny reaches behind her and pulls it closed.

"Thank you," I say before I take a successful sip of my coffee.

Tawny stays perched on the counter. "What are you calling a curse?"

Rye flips through a few pages of her journal and stops. She passes the journal to Talon, who just keeps bobbing his head yes. "You've seen one of these?" she asks, turning the book to each of us. The page has a hand-drawn sketch of a curse. Its accuracy of the angry face and razor-sharp teeth is uncanny. The drawing makes the curse's wings look like a weather-beaten faerie's wings.

"Two," Fin says. "There was one at two of the three locations we searched. We were looking for Chimmi. It was easy to assume Adria had been there, leaving behind the curse, especially when one of them had a tiny note that said it was from her."

"What are you calling a curse?" Tawny asks again.

The drawing has Fin transfixed, yet she speaks. "A curse is a physical embodiment of what normies like me believe is a supernatural power used to inflict harm or punishment. We deceive ourselves with the idea that it's bad luck, bad karma, coincidences, and that sort of thing when really, it's a creepy-looking bug entity that looks like an evil faerie."

Tawny hops off the counter and moves toward the journal. "I've seen those in the section of the tunnels I left last night," she says. "I didn't disturb them, and they didn't appear to care about me." Tawny turns to Rye. "We haven't mapped that area yet. It's an old area."

Rye gives a calculated nod. "I think Adria has been in the tunnels a lot longer than we thought."

Chapter 16

Rye spends a chunk of time asking Tawny questions. I'm not familiar with most of the things they discuss, since my exposure to the tunnel systems is limited. I shouldn't be surprised to learn that the maze of tunnels that runs under Lindsay is extensive, but I am.

Tawny describes crawling on her stomach, more like dragging herself, through a small opening in a collapsed section. Once through the opening, the tunnel on the other side is intact, decently preserved, and, as of now, partially sketched. Her voice has a steady, low-pitch. "I went through, Fin, because I have a job to complete."

"Listen, I'm all about commitment to a cause, but that sounds like suicide. Crawling through failed tunnels, alone, and without a way to communicate, is a death wish." I'm surprised with Fin's motherly tone. "So, you get through a hole, start mapping, and then what?"

"I finished rough mapping up to a fork in the tunnel. One side of the fork loops to where I crawled through the hole. The loop itself felt strange, like I was being watched, but I saw nothing. The other half of the fork, about a quarter of the way into that tunnel, was completely blocked. That was where the feeling of being watched was the most intense." Tawny grimaces and looks at Rye. "There were lots of tiny bug-like people on the surface of the debris. It looked like they were tunnelling in and out of minuscule gaps. It didn't feel right, so I bolted into the main section of the tunnel. In my hurry, though, I dislodged some debris, and the hole isn't passable for my return."

"Before we talk about whether the bug things can get through the same spot you did, let's talk about what they looked like, so we can be sure we're talking about a colony of curses," Fin says, like she's running the show.

"They moved in a blur, but when unmoving, they have mutilated grey wings and tiny humanish bodies."

"Yeap, that about does it," Fin says.

I can't stay quiet any longer. "How?"

"Kori, curses have existed as long as we have. There's evidence of curses in most, if not all, cultures." Fin stares at me, and she smiles. "Think about it. Broken mirror curses, voodoo dolls, curse tablets. You know, curse this and curse that." My wide-eyed stare changes to rapid blinking, and Fin just keeps talking. "Do you remember learning about those archeologists that were the first to open that ancient burial tomb? Within the next few years, they all had unexplained misfortunes. Some even died! And—"

Exasperated, I cut her off. "Fin!"

"What? I was curious, so I looked it up." She casts her eyes side to side, and she rushes her words. "Curses can be passed down for generations." She slams her hand over her mouth and closes her eyes.

I make a fist and thrust my pointer finger toward Fin, and I try to relax my tongue muscles as I speak. "Rye. Do you know why Tawny would find curses in the tunnels near The Society of the Blood Wind house?"

"Most, if not all, of the powerful Spellbinder families had generational curses. Different families dealt with their curses in different ways, but sacrificing a family member was the most successful method. Some families just left the curse to run its course, and eventually, it died out." Rye pauses. When she continues, her eyes are closed. "The Adelgriefs had a unique plan for their curses." She opens her eyes, but she isn't seeing us. "Unknown to anyone, I was in the tunnels the day they put their plan into motion. The chance of me being there at that time . . ." She shakes her head.

"Mallory Adelgrief was struggling with a string of

misfortunes which marked him as cursed. I don't know how Dolion and Nekane got him to willingly enter the tunnels, but he was there. I hid in the shadows at the tunnel's fork. With my vision magically magnified, I saw the curses go after him; their teeth were gnawing at the air. His scream made the curses's intent clear. I retracted my vision to avoid seeing them bite chunks from his flesh."

Rye's eyes are closed again, and her face is pale. Belamey straightens off the wall and steps toward her, laying his hand on her shoulder. She continues with his support. "I saw two shadows move past the entrance to my tunnel, and I heard their voices call the roof and the walls down to seal Mallory in with at least five curses."

The silence hangs until I break it. "I assume they weren't sealing the curses in to die."

Rye shakes her head. "If curses aren't distracted by the mischief they are causing, then they breed and populate fast. Think of a fly. It has a short life span, but it can lay five hundred eggs in batches of seventy-five to one hundred and fifty at a time."

I nod. *They are breeding an army of curses.* "How is Dolion planning to control them?"

Some of the colour is returning to Rye's skin. "They weren't worried about that detail. They knew they had time, years, to figure it out."

"The old tunnels are a perfect place," Fin muses. "Nobody used them, or so they thought," she flicks her hand toward Rye. "But it was close enough to their house for monitoring and control." Fin scrunches her face up. "But they can't be ready. Nekane is dead, and Dolion is dying. So, why are the curses coming out of Mallory's crypt?"

"Coincidence," I say without thinking it through. I feel my eyes flare at the absurdity of my word choice. Coincidence, a normie's word choice for explaining away magical things they refuse to accept.

Fin makes a gagging noise that draws everyone's eyes to her. She holds up her hand in a wait gesture. I glance at the clock and push my fingers into my temples. She continues dry-heaving. "What if the room is so full of curses that they are literally oozing out of the cracks?" She gags again.

I envision a room filled with flies eating and laying eggs in a corpse, and my compulsion is to retch with Fin. I push the image out of my head. "Adria obviously knows about the curses since she left some for us. Can she control them with Chimmi's power?"

Nobody answers, which is answer enough. My mouth is dry. I hunt for the coffee pot, sigh when I find it empty, and set about making a fresh brew. I'm aware of the murmur of continued conversation behind me while I stare at the coffeemaker, willing it to brew faster, but I don't register their words.

When I return to the table, Rye has a page from her book open, and she's showing the distance between the room Adria is in and the section of the tunnel where they murdered Mallory. The map scale is small. Rye explains that with no direct passage from one point to the other, a short distance can be long. I set the coffee pot down on the table. "So, it's two missions now," I say, lifting my cup to my lips. I blow on the hot liquid so I can inhale the bitter notes as steamy pillows.

"We're going to have to prioritize this shit," Fin says, pouring her cup of coffee. "There aren't enough of us to split into two teams."

When I open my eyes, the first thing I see is Tawny spinning the ring on her finger. "What are you thinking, Tawny?"

Startled, she snaps her eyes to me and lets go of her ring. "Adria and Chimmi are foremost, but I'm thinking of the tunnel system and how quickly to get from Adria to the room with the curses."

Rye stands. "We should go now."

"Without a plan?" I ask.

"We have a plan," Fin says. "Catch Adria, release Chimmi, and neutralize the curses."

"Talon, may I borrow the Willys MB?" Rye asks.

Talon bobs his head, hops to his feet, and produces the key from his robes with fast, jerky movements.

"Thank you," Rye says palming the keys. She closes her eyes and mumbles a few words. When her quiet words stop and her eyes open, she looks like a completely different person: spikey ash grey hair, light brown eyes with faint smile lines, and a thin mouth held in a soft smile. Maybe not entirely different. Physical form, height and weight, are similar between Rye and—she looks like Astrid Sapphirus! The Astrid we met and fought beside last year.

Fin's and my responses are simultaneous. We whip our heads at Belamey to spit out the same question. "Did you know?" One look at him, and it's clear that he didn't. I peek at Talon to see his response. He knows, but the knowledge is fresh.

Rye's voice comes out quiet, and her eyes don't stray from Belamey. "There are so many necessities to living a life in hiding. Astrid is one of my well-developed personas, personas that allow me to be close to the people who are important to me without being a danger to them or myself."

Belamey's resting face returns to its intense sadness. He gives a nod of acknowledgement and heads to the sunroom.

Fin reaches out and touches Rye's face. "How do you do it?" She breathes.

Rye is perceptive with her response. "There's one person who knows all my personas Fin, and without him, I wouldn't have had the strength to live this long." Before Fin can say anything else, Rye turns to Tawny. "Can you ride with me, please?" She doesn't wait for an answer. "Fin, please take everyone else in the Bronco and follow me."

This is our second time, within days, of racing in and out of the safe house without visiting with Talon. After an apology and a promise to return for a visit, I hug Talon and hurry out. I'm last to the truck. Rye is already turning out of the driveway as I hop into the box of the Bronco with Belamey. We hunker down under a blanket to block the winter chill. Belamey snakes his arm around me, pulling me tight to his side. The heat coming off his body is making my brain woozy. I swallow my thoughts of him without clothing on. *How can this man trigger a carnal response in me every time we're close?* I can't hear his chuckle, but I can feel the vibrations of it. I don't get a chance to question it because Fin rockets us forward, kicking up gravel, and we hit the road in a pocket of dust.

To distract myself from the proximity of Belamey's well-defined body, I magically amplified my hearing to listen inside the cab where Fin is dominating the conversation. "Is anyone else wondering why we're driving the opposite way from town and all of our archenemies? I'm in no hurry to enter the underground labyrinth and embrace the possibility of never seeing the light of day again, but I do fancy myself the title of a heroine, conqueror, vanquisher, victor, champion—"

"Perhaps you should be known forever as Fin, the boastful," I say.

Fin flashes me a smile. "Wrong. Call me Fin, the self-loving." As she's turning her eyes to the road, her gaze passes Lord Bradig. "But no name makes me complete like Fin, the reverent." She turns up the music and jams her foot on the accelerator.

I'm surprised when we turn up a pothole-filled driveway that leads toward an ancient-looking white farmhouse. It appears to be abandoned, but if that's the case, then who plows the snow? The windows are in darkness, and nothing moves, yet I sense we're being watched. Rye assesses us, turns without speaking, and marches into the snow-covered field toward an outbuilding. We trail her in silence, the hard snowy earth crunching with each step. She stops just before the building. It's leaning so far to the side that I'm sure one of Lord Bradig's hiccups could knock it over. Rye scans the area, searching. She shrugs and turns to us. "See that old well? That's your entry point."

Ten feet past the building is an aged cement well. It's set about one foot above the ground with a cover over it. Although I'm relieved we don't have to go into the building, I'm not happy to go down a well.

Rye doesn't wait for a response. By the time we follow her, she's cleared the far side of the structure. Suddenly, she drops into a cat-like crouch and throws up a shield dome. The response among us is instantaneous. Magic orbs, knives, and swords appear in our hands, none of which will do us any good unless Rye drops the surrounding shield. She has created a dome that keeps things out and keeps things in as well.

I'm searching the area for a threat when I see a bird racing toward us on long stick legs. The bottom half of this bird is black, and its top is a dirty white. Its beak is opening as it runs like it's screeching at us. Several long quills spread out on its head, giving the bird a crazed appearance. As it gets closer, Rye stands, and from behind, it looks like she flips through a handful of different appearances before landing back on Astrid. The bird reduces its pace, recognizing Rye.

Four and a half foot tall, the bird looks from this distance like it's wearing a tailcoat from the 1800s with black knee-high pants. Its quills give the impression of pens carried behind the ear. "The secretary," Fin says with awe.

I gape at her and the vulture-like bird. The bird stares at us from one eye on the side of its head. I'm shocked by the bright orange rimming its eyes. It stands tall with its chest out, watching us but listening to Rye. She exits the dome but leaves us trapped. Whatever passes between them is quick, and the dome disappears.

"Does it shift?" I mumble to Fin.

"You bet."

We draw in line with Rye, all staring at the secretary. I can't decide if the secretary is his nickname, job, or bird type. Before I can whisper my question to Fin, with her knowledge of Spellbinder birds, Rye clears her throat. The bird shifts its head so the side staring at us is looking at her. Rye waves her hand down the length of the bird's body, and up again. The bird tips its head, considering, then looks down at itself. It shifts into a wisp of a man. "Have they been prepped, Rye?"

"The tunnels are perilous. Trust Tawny, she'll keep

you safe."

Without preamble, he says, "You may enter." He turns and moves toward the well having read our urgency.

Griffin and Belamey move up beside him, and they shift the cover. Griffin climbs over the side and lowers himself out of sight.

"Why did we have to come so far out here to enter the tunnels, Rye?" Fin asks.

"There aren't too many ways into the tunnels without entering someone's home. With that in mind, this is the most direct and the shortest route to where you need to be."

"And the secretary?" She asks.

The secretary is busy explaining something to Belamey. Rye smiles as she watches. "His name is Archie Meek and he spends his time here. Meeks is his nickname. He's responsible for this entrance into the tunnels, scheduling who goes down and comes out, as well as when, and he keeps records. He's an old and trusted friend."

Intrigued, I ask, "Are all the entrances monitored this way?"

"All the ones that aren't inside a person's home, yes. But there aren't many left."

Lord Bradig, Belamey, and Tawny have disappeared into the well. Fin wanders over. She lets out an excited gasp and leaps in. My eyes go wide, and I tense, waiting for her scream and crash to the ground. I relax when I hear neither.

"Are you sure you can't come, Rye?"

"No, Kori." Rye looks to Meeks. He's beckoning for me to hurry into the well.

Sighing, I walk over and peek in. Nobody is in sight. I expect to see a bucket system or climbing ropes to carry me down. What I see is a quick drop to a winding staircase that curves the circumference of the well. The drop isn't far enough to make shifting worth the effort. I climb over the side. The cement is freezing against my fingers as I hang with my body pressed against the inside wall of the well. I hover there for a few seconds and then open my fingers. My body grazes the wall, and I taste the dust from it as I drop to the platform at the top of the stairs.

Once I feel steady on my feet, I glance upwards to see the cover being closed. I don't know how I keep myself from pitching off the staircase when Tawny speaks from the stairway. She hadn't been there when I dropped, and I didn't hear her approach.

"Follow me, no extra light." She turns and starts down the stairs.

When we reach the bottom, we're deep underground. It's a stagnant environment. Griffin has a faint glow orb that makes us look like shadows in the darkness. I'm about to form a bright glow orb when Tawny spins on me. "Dim light is best. Let's not wake anything that doesn't want to be woken. Or worse, wake something we prefer asleep."

Fin's voice is strangled when it echoes out of the darkness. "How is one option worse than the other? I

want nothing to wake. I don't want to see anything—
"

"Fin, put your knives away, so you don't accidentally stab us," Belamey says.

Chapter 17

The dim light barely casts a glow. Without being able to see the surface of the walls or the expanse of the tunnel, the darkness is overwhelming. It isn't an oppressive feeling, but more of a hunger. The dark— or things in the dark—are hungry. Our group's silence does nothing to ease my strange lingering feelings of discomfort.

I amplify my hearing, but there's no sound beyond our footsteps, breathing, and Lord Bradig's sporadic hiccups. I can't say what tipped me off, but without conscious thought, I wheel to face the tunnel and drop to a knee in one fluid motion. Tawny's warning about light can be damned. As I spin, I release a flare orb down the tunnel, throwing a clear shield up to seal us off from whatever is approaching.

The golden light from the flare illuminates an underground hell. In the spots where they're visible, the damp stone walls are covered with fungi. Roots have pierced the roof and walls, creating thick patches of webbing that have drastically decreased the tunnel's width. Seeing the brief glimpse of the tunnel leaves me wondering how we walked through the space without feeling the tickle of root ends on our persons. The light is fading out when a curse slams into the shield. Its sharp teeth chomp vigorously.

The flare orb has stopped providing light, leaving only Tawny's dim orb to see with. Everyone has moved toward my shield to get a better look at this solo curse, struggling to attack us. There's no time to consider the implications of this curse's appearance because a dark, wiggling profile drops from the roof. It snatches at the curse as it drops, tearing it off the shield, still biting. It hits the ground with a soft wet thump, the curse is nowhere to be seen, and the shape moves out of sight in a blur.

"Did a fast-moving blur of *what the fuck was that* just drop from above and eat the curse?" Fin says quietly. Her words are over-pronounced.

That creeping feeling of hunger has meaning now. Shivers run over my whole body.

Tawny's voice is urgent. "We need to go."

"What was that?" I ask, straining to see into the darkness.

"That was a murk salamander." Tawny's voice and her dim light are moving away. "We need to go."

Fin's voice gives away her facial expression. I know

her eyes are little accusing slits, giving Tawny a questioning glare. "It was an intense moving shape, but it was pretty small. Why do I feel like there's more to your urgency?"

Tawny doesn't stop moving, and she doesn't answer. It's Griffin's low rough voice that fills the tunnel. "That was a baby. There will be more than a solo hungry little one."

My eyes scan the roof and walls, seeing only darkness, but knowing there's more there. "Babies usually mean there's a mother close by."

"The big ones are called murk monsters," Griffin says. Because he's beside me, I see the shadow of orbs form on his hands.

"Why murk monster?" Fin asks, her knives appear. "Is it just the supernatural aspect of it?"

I'm holding the shield behind us, dragging it as we move deeper into the tunnel. A dark shadow plunges past my eyes. If it wasn't close to my face, or if I blinked, I wouldn't have seen it. I whip my left hand over my head, drawing my shield into a movable dome with us inside. With my right hand, I fling an immobilizing orb at the ground in front of my feet, praying that I hit the murk salamander and not anyone's toes. My motions divert the group, causing Tawny to return.

"Dropped within centimetres of my nose. I think I immobilized it," I say, straining to see the ground.

Tawny crouches with her dim light. A salamander, its colour the definition of darkness, lies unmoving.

There isn't anything about it that's outlandish at first glimpse. The wet sheen on its skin gives it an almost pretty appearance.

Fin puts her foot down on its tail. "Just in case. I'd hate for it to be tricking us," she says. "Murk as in darkness, difficult to see . . ." Her voice trails off as we crouch together to have a closer look.

"It doesn't have eyes," I breathe, shocked.

"Doesn't need them in the darkness. Its other senses are sharpened," Griffin says.

Fin bolts into a stand moving one foot and leaving the other extended to keep its tail pinned. "Onc this size couldn't hurt us, right?"

"It chews or swallows smaller insects, but with prey our size, it bites on and its tongue burrows into the flesh to drain the fluids. The babies would share us as a meal."

The murk salamander gives a cry and bolts, leaving its tail behind. Lord Bradig's axe flashes out, ending with a sickening crunch. "Got the wee sleeven." Before he can start hiccupping, a clicking sound fills the air. The clicking gets fast and turns into a shriek.

"And mommy?" Fin says quietly.

Griffin peers into the darkness. "Mommy is big enough to eat us whole."

"Time to go," Tawny yells.

We charge after her. I keep the dome held in place as we move, there's a marginal chance it'll have an effect on the murk monster chasing us.

"There are strange things here that you won't find outside of these tunnels. Many of them were creations, mutated creatures, used to guard the tunnels or things in them." Tawny's words are breathless as she races blindly forward. "They can't come out of the tunnels. Someone magically bonded them to the space, but they live and thrive here."

The murk monster is clicking again and another is replying.

"We just need to reach the next junction of the tunnel before it catches us," she calls with a burst of speed.

"What'll that do?" Fin hollers over the clicking.

"Murk monsters are bonded to the tunnels connected to the well entrances. They can only travel so far."

We're moving so fast a wave of panic hits me. *How can Lord Bradig's short legs keep up with us?* I don't see him. "Where's Lord Bradig?"

I almost don't hear Belamey as two shrieks echo through the tunnel. "He's with me."

Belamey is running in front of me, but I can't see Lord Bradig. I push my legs to propel myself closer. He blinks into sight, piggybacked by Belamey and then disappears again. I hear his voice, "Tell her."

Belamey doesn't modify his powerful steps. "Lord Bradig is with me as a way to preserve his energy for any upcoming battles."

My connection to the dome jars violently. I look up to see the silhouette of a murk monster equal to my size, a living shadow trying to cling to the top of the dome with its four legs swimming and its strange-toed feet flexing for grip. Its body is snake-like, and its tail slides in that familiar s-shaped pattern as it slips down the dome.

I didn't design the dome to push things, and we're moving too fast to stop as a group. The dome allows items to move in the front, travel through, and continue out. The murk monster is inside with us. It's thrashing, trying to get its feet under it. Tawny is knocked down, and she's flattened herself to the ground as the murk monster's tail flicks over her body. Lord Bradig is pinned against the wall of the dome, having chosen this as one of his energy-worthy battles. He's chopping at the murk monster's toes and jumping over its leg as it flails in response. The toes are regrowing as quickly as he's lopping them off.

"Don't waste your knives," Griffin tells Fin with a calmness that's ridiculous amid the chaos. "They won't pierce the adult's skin." They press against the opposite side of the dome from Lord Bradig. The orbs Griffin formed earlier cacoon him and Fin. The weaves suggest he has blocked their smell and sound.

Belamey, muscles taut, is staring at a second murk monster, arching its tail up and shrieking. I let the dome vanish. I pound an orb into the ground that lets out a sound, smell, and vibration that won't overwhelm our human senses, but that I hope will overwhelm the murk monster's sharpened ones. Tawny has increased the brightness of her orb, illuminating a fork in the tunnel just ahead.

The murk monster that slid down the dome is writhing on the ground, struggling to control its parts. The second murk monster is rigid, like its senses are temporarily inundated. We're racing past the second one on both sides of it when its tail flicks, catching Fin's foot. She hits the ground and corrects with a roll as I jump the tail that's now flicking in my direction. I race into the right fork as Fin rolls into the left. I spin to follow her but grind to a halt with my arms flailing. Both murk monsters are facing this fork in the tunnel. Their limbs are tense as they wait to pounce.

"They can't come into the forks," Tawny says as she materializes beside me. "On either side."

I swallow. The flicking of their tails is mesmerizing. Tawny's hand flashes in front of my face. "Don't watch their tails. They use them to transfix their prey."

I blink, shake my head, glance at Tawny, and then into our new tunnel. Everyone except Fin is on this side. "What about Fin?" I turn to the opening, calculating if I can make the jaunt into the other fork. The murk monsters are clicking, doing calculations of their own.

"Fin?" I holler.

"I'm okay. It's sparkly in here. Is it over there?"

I look at Tawny as I yell to Fin. "Did you hit your

head?"

"Don't touch the sparkles, Fin." Tawny hollers. When there's no response, Tawny calls again, "Fin, tell me you didn't touch the sparkles."

"I didn't, but I want to."

"Don't. I'll explain later. For now, know that it wouldn't end well. Do you understand?"

"I understand enough. Now what?"

I stay quiet and let Tawny talk. "Now, you follow that tunnel, and we follow this one."

"I don't like that idea," Fin yells.

"Me neither," I hiss.

The murk monsters haven't changed position. It's eerie how they know our exact location without the ability to see us. Sightless, their lives in darkness have honed their sense of sound and smell into a deadly weapon. They're no longer clicking. If Tawny's dim light winked out, their presence would be undetectable until it was too late.

Tawny regulates her volume. "We don't have a choice. Murk monsters are almost impossible to kill. One or all of us would die trying. We're lucky nobody died already. Plus, there are two of them. They're starving, angry, and locked onto us like we're homing beacons, so we can't just slip by."

"Guys?" Fin yells.

Tawny ignores her and continues talking. "The sparkles add a soft glow to that tunnel. She can see with no light. The sparkles are that fork's danger, if touched you crystallize. As long as she doesn't touch them, she's safe."

"Blazing hell!" I gage the wall and stomp my foot. "Do these tunnels meet up?"

Tawny is walking into the depth of our tunnel when she answers. "Eventually."

I make a pathetic effort to square my shoulders. "Fin?"

"Kori?"

"Fin, you need to follow your tunnel and meet up with us at the other end." Silence answers me. "Fin?"

"Okay."

"Tawny said that the sparkles will give you a soft light to see by. But Fin?"

"Yeah."

"Don't touch the sparkles."

She doesn't answer, but I hear her feet moving away. With Tawny's light no longer illuminating the area, I glare in the direction of the murk monsters, only able to assume they're there. Cursing, I turn and follow the others, wondering what fresh hell awaits us.

Chapter 18

I push my way to the front of the group so I can walk with Tawny. "What can we expect to find in this tunnel?"

She gives me a sideways glance. "Bats," she says, dimming the light of her orb so that we're almost in darkness.

I cast my eyes to the roof, but it's too dark to see if there are hanging winged creatures. "Just regular bats?"

She shrugs. I drop back, and walk in silence. Periodically, I reach out with my ability to sense living matter. My first concern is to check on Fin. I sense her instantly. She's a jumble of sexual excitement, bubbly wit, fierce passions, and versatility. I also take a few minutes to assess the life forms within our immediate vicinity. Awareness dawns. That unpleasant feeling, that unseen danger, from Just

Flavours and then from the jungle, its here. I hadn't made the connection in our apartment or at the safe house because I hadn't been using my sensing ability. It isn't a technique I use regularly, so I inadvertently forget about it. "Stop," I hiss, reaching forward to grab Tawny. My halt brings everyone to a stop.

"What?" she asks without moving a muscle.

"I sense a small life form just up ahead. It's a curse."

Lord Bradig brushes past my leg. His eyes glow like a built-in flashlight when he looks up at me. I didn't think I would ever find another creature whose eyes glow brighter than mine in the darkness.

"Lord Bradig, what are you doing?"

"Kori, the renowned, you said there is a curse, and that is a job for Lord Bradig, the superlative. Besides," he says, without stopping, "I have a need for a devilish wee snack."

He disappears outside of our dim light, but the glow of his eyes marks his movement, making it obvious when he stops. There's a sucking sound and an explosion of hiccups, followed by a low belch. "The wee sleeven won't be a bother to us now," Lord Bradig says, waiting for us to reach him.

Beyond us, I sense no other living matter in the tunnel, either in front or behind. "I can't feel bats, Tawny."

Stepping up to me, she searches my face. "You won't." She lifts her light orb above her head. Barely visible on the roof, many strange shapes hang. They're so still, and there are so many of them. If I didn't know what I was looking at, I'd assume they were stalactites.

"Why?" I ask, casting my eyes to Tawny. She lowers her light and looks me in the eye. "Eternal sleep. Another tormented creature forced to guard the tunnels." She tips her head questioningly. When I just blink at her, she nods, turns, and walks. I'm forced to stay with her to hear her words. "A kind of sleep that subdues internal functions, so the organism is almost dead."

I hear the play on another normie belief, the idea of eternal sleep being death. *It can't be that simple.* "How does the organism wake?"

"If it wakes, it wakes angry and hungry. But it only wakes when triggered. Triggers depend on the creature and the purpose of the eternal sleep. Throwing your light orb here could be devastating for us."

I choose to ignore the bulk of her words. "And if it doesn't get triggered?"

"Death." Tawny shrugs. "Eventually."

I cast my eyes sideways to see if she's joking. She's walking and looking straight ahead. Nothing in her demeanour suggests she's anything but honest. My mouth feels dry as my brain rolls through more questions. "Can all organisms be placed in eternal sleep?"

"Yes. Even humans," Tawny says like she can't

believe I'm asking.

I look at the darkened roof. "Who did this?" My voice is so quiet I can hardly hear myself. "It seems so . . ." I flail for words.

"Does it sound so different from binding creatures forever in the darkness?" Tawny's exasperation is prominent in her voice. She takes a deep breath, and when she speaks again, her voice is level. "We aren't here to judge, Kori. That's not our purpose. Plus, how do we judge things we don't fully know or understand?"

Silence, the only sounds come from our footfalls and Lord Bradig's sporadic hiccups. I shift my focus to the changes in the surroundings. The floor, covered in chunks of rock and loose dirt, has shifted to flat random shaped stones, a sophisticated walkway. It's clear this area of the tunnel is better preserved; even the walls and roof are in better shape. The stale smell is more earthy. *We must be closer to our intended destination.*

"When does this tunnel meet up with Fin's?" I ask Tawny.

Her pace doesn't wane. "No, idea."

I'm casting out with my senses when Tawny answers. I'm about to snap when I feel something moving like a wall toward us. A sensation of hundreds of life forms. With there being so many, the unpleasant feeling I typically sense is marked with a dark playfulness, a malevolent poison. "Curses," I whisper, frantically searching my brain for a way to save us from the wave about to swarm. I draw a dome around us. "They can't leave the tunnel," I say to nobody in particular.

The air stirs. I blink when the air currents become visible as a baby blue, and petrichor fills my nostrils. Lord Bradig's body sways with the rhythm of his hands. He's turning a manufactured wind like a large ball caught in his grasp. As he turns it, the baby blue gives way to a darker blue, with greys and blacks, and they all emit light. The intense smell of rain takes on hints of damp earth and wet grass. I release the dome. Lord Bradig's wind grows until his arms are swirling in their shoulder sockets as he continues to build the wind's power. Everyone's focus is on him as his wind pulls, trying to suck us in.

The tunnel vibrates with the thrashing of wings as the hive of curses barrels toward us. The continuous humming echoes in the small space. It's impossible to imagine the dinginess of the tunnels becoming darker, but the swarm of curses creates a blackness so complete it's like everything stopped existing and fell into a void.

Lord Bradig releases the wind. The air currents spiral toward the curses. Its light illuminates a dark solid ball, making individual curses visible as they tumble and roll over one another in their frenzied approach. The airspeed increases, creating a sound of its own, a howl that breaks into a deafening roar. It tears through their ranks, battering some against the walls, floor, and roof as it forces them backwards down the tunnel. The howling fades. I don't believe that it's because the wind dies out, but instead because it has travelled a distance from us.

There can't be anything, friendly or not, in the tunnel in front of us. Belamey's thoughts must be the same as mine because he throws a bright orb down the tunnel. The light displays the carnage of curses. None moving. Even the roof has been purged of its eternally sleeping bats. Frantic, I cast out for Fin. My hands are trembling and I press my palms to my heart when I sense her, the same as she was when I checked her last.

"Thank you, Lord Bradig," Belamey says. Lord Bradig's body bounces with his hiccups.

I spin on Tawny, not trying to hide my anger. "What do you mean you don't know when this tunnel meets up with the other one?" I feel Belamey move beside me. His body heat would be welcome if my blood wasn't already boiling me from the inside.

"Easy, Firecracker," he breathes.

Tawny doesn't look the least bit phased. She actually has the audacity to look like I'm overreacting. I step toward her, ready to shake the look off her teenage face, but Belamey's arm fastens to my waist, securing me against him. His lips brush my ear as he whispers, "Fin will be okay. You and I both know it. Tawny's role is to get us to Adria and Chimmi. That's what she's doing."

I suck a deep breath, take a long blink, and look at Tawny. She has rearranged the features on her face to look neutral. "Appreciate her effort," Belamey whispers. I'm not sure if he means her effort to get us this far or her effort to alter her facial expression so I don't change it for her.

"Kori, I'm sorry. Fin will be okay in that tunnel. I've travelled it. It'll eventually lead to the same place as us, but it won't hook directly into this tunnel. If I had told you when we first separated, you would've tried to get past the murk monsters to get to Fin. I have my orders. Letting you kill yourself or any of us isn't part of them." She's rubbing the ring on her middle finger using her thumb on the same hand. I'm sure if she wasn't controlling the orb so closely, she would spin the ring with her other hand. Something about the action makes me wonder where her orders are coming from. Her eyes follow my gaze to her ring, and she stops fiddling with it. "If we keep our pace, this tunnel should be shorter."

I know she's right, but I don't want anyone else knowing I agree. "*Should be* shorter?"

She nods. "I haven't actually travelled this side of the tunnel. It's mapped in the old records, and I've studied those."

Belamey releases his grip on my waist. I know the hesitance in his movement has nothing to do with concern for Tawny. I suppress my internal acknowledgement that I didn't push him away or resist his arm. Tawny thinks my eye roll is at her comment.

Her *it smells* face scrunches up even more.

"What?"

I don't correct her assumption. "What else do the maps say is in this tunnel, Tawny?"

She shrugs, indifferent. "I didn't study that part as hard." She stops walking, increasing her orb's brightness. "Shouldn't matter."

I follow the direction of her gaze. Our tunnel branches into four sections. "Tawny?"

"We go this way." Tawny advances toward a solid section of the wall. I scan for signs of magic, remembering Rye's comments about secret tunnels, but I can't see anything. Tawny passes straight through the wall, and we follow. It isn't a tunnel we enter. It's a hallway that's angled up so steeply that stairs would have made more sense.

"Tawny?"

"This leads to the room above where Adria and Chimmi are."

"Above?"

Her head moves up and down. "Above. We're going to be dropping in!"

Chapter 19

"When we drop into the room, the first person will have the element of surprise, but then what?" I ask, eyeballing the hole in the floor. It's wide enough for a person to fall through. It wouldn't end well for a normie, though, because a magically controlled descent is required.

"The plan is simple," Tawny says. "You're dropping first. The way I understand things, you and Adria have some unfinished business. But before you drop, Belamey and Griffin are going to bind her magic so you can battle it out normie style. Or you can just blast her with your magic. Their bind will be stronger once they have a visual. For now, it will be enough that they know she's there. Can you do that thing and sense her?"

Irritated, I remember how easy it was for Belamey to bind me last year. If I'm being honest, I'd acknowledge my jealousy over Adria's strength and knowledge. It requires two Spellbinders to focus their efforts on her to keep her magic bound. Belamey reads it on my face. "You'd be the same, if not stronger, Kori. You're no longer ignorant or resistant to your magic." He pauses. "You've come a long way, but let's be honest, magic still isn't completely instinctual."

I shoot a burn-in-hell look at Belamey, which gets me a devilish smile in return. So he can't read the effect that his smile has on my pulse and breathing, I turn away. Reaching out, I feel two life forms. "Chimmi and Adria are in the room."

"Get these on her wrists." Tawny holds up two thick elastic bands linked with a tiny metal jump ring. The smile on my face is fake. The notion that elastic and thin metal can control a Spellbinder of any magical strength is ridiculous. But I've learned things aren't always what they seem, especially when magic is involved. "That leaves Lord Bradig and me to find Chimmi, remove the silver dominance coupler, and get him somewhere safe."

I raise my eyebrows and nod at her *this-will-be-simple* attitude. Belamey, Griffin, and Lord Bradig remain silent as I take the farcical handcuffs and cram them into my pocket noting their weightlessness. I step to the hole's edge and weave an invisible mixture of fast-moving air currents trapped in a pattern that rolls in and over itself. Mixed into the currents are teeny water droplets and small ice crystals. It's woven together in a web that makes it dense enough to keep me from falling through it for a limited period, an air cloud. My mass will force it toward the ground at a controlled pace. I look at Belamey.

He nods. "We got her."

Without giving myself a chance to think better of it, I step onto the cloud. The initial pressure of my weight drops it fast into the darkness of the hole, but after that, the speed levels out. I feel like I'm floating down instead of dropping. It's dark. I keep my arms tight at my sides, not wanting to hit anything sticking out from the wall. There's only darkness below me. When I look up, the entrance to the hole isn't visible either. I sigh at my limited knowledge. I decide to keep my gaze down so that I'm prepared when I finally reach the bottom.

When I see light under me, I form stun orbs. I loosen the weave of the cloud and plunge into the room, scanning for the red of Adria's hair. Before I hit the floor, I launched my orbs at her. I make a direct hit to her head and chest, thinking that this fight will be over before it starts. The orbs stun her, but they don't immobilize. *She partially blocked the effect of the orb. She isn't fully blocked from her magic.* The surprise on her face from my attack quickly turns to frustration when she can't form magic to retaliate. Belamey is already in the room.

Adria wastes no time. She tucks her head and dives at my waist. The force of her tackle sets our momentum, and we go down hard. Her perfume clogs my airway as we roll across the ground. We break apart and get our feet under us, facing off with our fists up to protect our faces, and our bodies are bladed. We circle, looking for an opening or a weakness. I consider hitting her with a stun orb, but I can't give in to my desire to best her in combat. Getting the cuffs on her without using my magic seems like a fair fight. I trust that Lord Bradig and Tawny will get to Chimmi. The thought of him draws my attention to Adria's right hand. The ring is there, but now I've given her the opportunity she was waiting for. She comes in swinging.

I side-step, but I barely block her punch to the side of my head. Bringing my arm up to shield my head opened my side, and she lands a good hit. The air escapes my lungs forcefully. I rally by driving my knee up. I don't make contact, but I create space between us to follow through with a kick at Adria's midsection. Now it's her turn to expel air explosively. It doesn't slow her, and she launches at me with another tackle. Tawny, Lord Bradig, and Chimmi are the last things I see as Adria and I tumble into an adjoining tunnel.

We're on a floor of loose gravel. My eyes water in response to the dusty air. The sharp points on various rocks dig into my body as we grapple. There's grit in my mouth. My patience is thinning with the whole situation. Adria has me pinned, throwing punches. I have my head buried in my arms to avoid them. Realizing we're close to the wall, I use my feet to walk partway up the wall and lever my body, knocking Adria off balance. As I roll over top of her, I imagine myself being an angry wildcat. She's face down, and I have her arm trapped behind her. With a smile, I ram my knee into the small of her back. I keep her arm pulled up enough to maintain control of her while I put the first shackle on.

The loose elastic of that first cuff makes a harsh sucking sound as it cinches tight. When Adria realizes what I just slipped on her wrist, she panics, bucking. I push my weight onto her keeping her pinned. My other leg, shin positioned for stability, runs flat behind me so that I'm not thrown off. I need to gain control of her other arm, so I crank her other arm up hard. Her bucking stops, and she lets out a snarl. I hold the arm tight with one hand as I reach for the other.

I know there's no point in giving her verbal commands. She won't comply. As soon as she feels me shift my weight to reach for her free hand, she bucks again. I topple and lose my grip on her cuffed arm. I reposition so that I fall on top of her, and I move fast to grab her head, bring it up, and bang it down with enough force to knock her silly. Grabbing her free hand, I ram it through the second cuff. It pulls tight with the same sucking noise.

Rolling away from Adria, I wipe the sweat from my forehead. It feels gritty and scratches my skin. I sit against the wall, watching her while I catch my breath. My pulse is loud in my ears. When Adria stirs, I scrub my hand over my face and climb to my feet. I yank her up and march her into the main room.

Tawny and Bradig are crouched down. I can't see Chimmi, but I know they're working on helping him. My hand is still on Adria's arm. I whip her body sideways so that her hands are visible. She's trying to move her thumb and ring finger, but the handcuffs are limiting her movements. Latching onto her left thumb, I lever it enough to make her squeal. Her hands arch, and I slide the ring off her right pointer finger. She struggles, but I just bend that thumb a bit more and yank the ring off.

The combo rings jingle in my palm. Whether the removal of it from Adria's hand was the catalyst or the timing was a coincidence, I don't know, but the silver ball in Chimmi's neck pulls free from his flesh, displaying a long thin needle that had been forced deep into him.

I scan the room for a genuine look. The first thing I notice is that the hole in the roof isn't visible. I shift my head, but I can't see any faint wisps of magic concealing the opening. There are four tunnels. One looks like it's a newer—or at least maintained— tunnel. Then there's a sparkly tunnel and the one Adria and I were fighting in. Rye's symbol marks the fourth. The long-reaching society hands, or sideways flames, with fading swirls naturally decorate the stone wall. This tunnel has a vintage wooden door covering it.

The door looks out of place. When it swings open, it's even more unusual. Dolion steps into the room, tall and proud. A man who refuses to let age wear him down. I see a likeness in his aged face that reminds me of Nekane and Belamey. A shadow hovers over him, and then the bald, wiry form of Kyson appears. Kyson bristles like a hungry cat that just found a room full of mice. Dolion's face displays his surprise, but it's quickly replaced by another look as his eyes land on Adria.

From the corner of my eye, I see Lord Bradig and Tawny move to hide Chimmi behind them. Their job doesn't change even though our situation has. Their goal is to get Chimmi to a place of safety. The silence in the room is surreal. Time stands still. Dolion strikes out first. Like a snake, his hand shoots out from his side in Belamey's direction. I see the fingers of Dolion's hand. His four fingers are level as he pinches his thumb flat against them. When his arm reaches its full extension, his fingers and thumb pull apart, creating a mouth-like impression from which a thick weave of cloudy yellow colour flies. My eyes go wide. He has conjured and thrown venom.

Belamey is so surprised by the arrival of his grandfather that he isn't quick enough with his reaction. The shield he weaves and throws in front of himself keeps the bulk of the venom from hitting him, but not all of it. What hits him connects with his face. His eyes are closed when it hits, but it doesn't matter. His muscles go into spasms, his whole body convulsing. As the spasms increase in intensity, his balance goes, and he pitches forward, shaking. I see Griffin toss a weave of air under him to cushion his fall. The weave remains under him as his body gives one last violent shudder. Griffin moves to Belamey, but his focus is on Dolion and Kyson. If they attack at once, neither Griffin nor Belamey will survive.

Adria bumps me. Her body pushes against mine as she brushes behind me, snapping my attention from Belamey. Adria is trying to put distance between herself and Dolion. The way her body is tense suggests fear. She locks her focus on him, her expression one of sheer hate. There's equal hostility in his stare. I see the weaves of magic forming on Dolion's hands. It isn't a smooth formation; it cracks and breaks. His face strains and looks pained, then shifts to complete surprise. The magic weaves just vanish. His hands race to his chest as his legs give out. The sound of his knees hitting the floor is accompanied by the crunching of bone. His body makes a loud bang as he hits the ground face first, unmoving.

If things felt surreal before, they feel completely unreal now. Adria moves. She bends like she's trying to get a better view of Dolion. She makes a strangled sound, like a laugh that's choked off. She straightens herself and this time gives a very clear bark of laughter. My eyes bulge. She angles her body at Dolion and starts full-out laughing.

Her outburst has broken the standstill. Griffin

drops to Belamey's side, working a healing weave I don't have time to focus on because Kyson's eyes lift from the lifeless form of Dolion and fix on Adria. The way his lifeless cobalt blue eyes lock on her reminds me of his twin, and I have to remind myself Kieran died last year. I battle with the sense of helplessness that threatens to creep over me. They trained Kyson to kill. He lives to kill, unlike Kieran, who was apt at torturing a person to the brink of death without letting them fall into that abyss. I shake myself. *Focus.*

Kyson's scarred face becomes my focal point. Slinking toward Adria and me, his intent is clear. I realize I could push her forward, sacrifice her to buy time for the rest of us to respond or escape, but that isn't my style. I shove her behind me a bit too roughly, and she loses her balance. Her laughter doesn't stop even as she hits the floor. *Blazing hell, she's lost her marbles.* I shield her and myself. Paralytic stun orbs form on my hands without thought. Although I would like to cleanse the earth of Kyson, that's not how I operate. My orb design should knock him unconscious, but given his strength and protection, it may only daze him, so I add in a paralytic to make him incapable of movement.

Kyson's preoccupation with Adria is fascinating. He has eyes only for her. He almost has me convinced that it's only him and her in the room. Her laughter is grating. I flick a finger behind me in her direction, using a simple magic weave to mute her voice, and in the silence, I find success. Regardless, I'm sure her body and mouth are shaking.

Kyson lunges at the same time that Adria's silent laughter makes her flail into my legs. My orbs sail out of my hands, but only one hits Kyson. It clips his left shoulder. I brace for the impact of him diving into me. Something zings past my head, chased by two more fast-moving blurs. *Fin!* The sparkling tunnel is at my back. I don't shift my position, fearing that one of her knives will hit me. The three she threw are minis. Highly accurate but unlikely to kill. All three stab into the flesh of Kyson's shoulder on the side the orb clipped. The force plowing into the same shoulder drives him off balance. He stumbles off course.

Kyson makes an odd noise that's out of place with his stumble. Then he roars, his hands swatting and swinging. His left side is cumbersome and uncoordinated. My eyes bulge when I see a curse on the left side of his neck, and then a hole in his flesh. The curse burrowed into him. Based on his frantic actions, more curses that I can't see must be sinking themselves into him. *Scouts, like the one Lord Bradig ate in the tunnel before we were almost swarmed.*

The room fills with an echoing vibration, a low, continuous humming that's impossible not to be cognizant of. Now a high buzz, it's coming from the tunnel Adria and I rolled into and it's growing closer. I peer into it and swallow hard. I can see a large angry black cloud speeding toward us. "Smoke and ashes," I whisper.

"No," Fin says. "A swarm of curses sent to devour our flesh and devastate the world."

Chapter 20

Rye steps into the room from the sparkling tunnel. She looks like herself. No disguise. Her eyes sweep the room, taking in Belamey's unconscious form before looking at Tawny. Something unspoken passes between them. Tawny closes her eyes and nods, very solemn and final.

Rye positions herself in the path of the black mass of billowing curses. After a brief pause, she takes four very defined steps. She plants her feet wide, raises her arms, and tilts her head. A high-pitched buzzing sound emanates from her. The wall of curses hits her body, but not one passes by. Her buzzing turns into a scream as the number of visible curses dwindles.

I can't see the front of her body, but as the pitch of her scream changes to one of pain and sheer terror, I understand. She has called the curses into her, trapping them there to save us. The sight of her slight frame inflating as the curses fill her body is too horrific to look away from. It's like I'm in a hypnotized state of morbid magnetism. Her body distends. Her skin, where not covered by clothing, shows the movement of the curses.

When the curse's buzzing is gone, Rye's scream echoes in the space before fading to a moan as she slumps to the floor. Fin and I race to her side. We aren't sure what to do. Her body is unrecognizable. "She's going to burst," Fin says, choking on her words. "What do we do?"

Tawny steps forward.

My blood boils. "You knew what she would do, right? That was the look you shared. How could you let her?"

Fin's head whips toward us. Her eyes dart between us but stop on me. I know my face is turning red because I can feel the heat of my anger burning from the inside out. Fin moves so that she's in between Tawny and me. She starts asking questions to refocus the situation. "Can we save her? What will happen with those curses in there?"

Tawny is watching Rye's body and nibbling her lip. "The curses will be asleep from the internal heat. The initial warmth lulls them, but they'll wake, and when they do, they'll feast and lay eggs in whatever is left of her."

I know there isn't a delicate way to give that explanation, but it feels insensitive. I cast my eyes at Belamey, who is still unmoving. At the moment, that's a blessing, but if he wakes, how do we explain what happened to his mother? Tawny startles me when she speaks. "I'll help Belamey first."

"You can help him?" Fin asks without missing a beat. "And you can help Rye, too?"

The mention of Belamey draws my eyes in that direction. *What if I lose him?* The tunnel door leading into the house upstairs swings shut, muffling a bang on the other side. I scan the room. Fin's small knives are on the floor with two smashed curses, presumably from Kyson's neck. *Were there only two attacking him?* Kyson used the commotion from the curses to collect Dolion's body and escape into the tunnel. I make a mental note to check the door, but first, I return my unrest to Tawny.

Her pinched facial expression doesn't change. She shifts her eyes to Chimmi. Twisting the ring on her finger, she makes a series of strange noises as she watches him. Chimmi's head tips to the side, listening. Tawny goes quiet and crouches down. Chimmi wobbles across the room toward her as fast as he can.

"What's happening?" Fin whispers.

I blink and keep watching.

"Chimmi and Tawny are bonded," Lord Bradig says. He bows in their direction and holds the position. None of us move or speak. When he stands again, he's looking at Tawny. "My apologies for not recognizing you sooner, Princess of the Green Fields."

"Lord Bradig, the superlative, you do not need to

make apologies to me." Tawny says. "I tested the strength of my disguise when I said I received my ring from one of your species. I knew then that even you couldn't see through it. So, I apologize to you, Lord Bradig, the superlative, for the trickery."

Fin looks at me and mouths her words, "Are you as confused as I am?"

I nod without taking my eyes off Tawny.

Chimmi scurries up Tawny's body stopping on her shoulder. "That's the spot, is it, Chimmi?" she asks. Chimmi makes no sound or movement. She nods and moves toward Belamey.

Griffin stands to give her a workspace. Sweeping up and down Belamey's body, her hands work in a blur pulling a cloudy yellow venom out. Her eyes close, and her expression hardens. The magic is resisting her efforts to remove it. His body arches off the floor as the magic fights to hold him. Tawny doesn't give in. Her mouth works in silent words as her hands move fast in what looks like a frantic pattern. The magic suddenly releases. Belamey crumples. Tawny has captured the magic between her hands, and she's agitating it. As she works, a pale cloud separates from the venom and dissipates in the air until what she's churning is clear yellow, no longer cloudy. Her hands slow, and when they stop moving, she's holding a puddle of yellow liquid.

"It's no longer toxic," she explains as she discards it on the ground. She locks eyes with me. "He's healed, but he won't wake for a few hours." Without waiting for me to respond, she moves toward Rye but addresses her next question to Chimmi. "Are you ready for this, friend?"

I look down at Belamey. The paleness of his skin warms to a soft pink. His breathing carries the rhythm of a sleeper. I can see his eyes darting behind his closed eyelids. His expression tightens and his body clenches. Alarmed, I crouch beside him sliding my hand into his. *When all this is over, I need to prioritize you and me. No more delays because of my history.* The warmth from his hand is a comfort, and it must be to him, too, because he relaxes.

I watch as Tawny removes the silver tree ring from her finger. She strokes its green leaves and examines her hand without the ring. When she looks up, she locks eyes first with me and then with Fin. "Make sure Rye remembers to not take this ring off. It'll be what sustains her health. Please, tell her." Tawny pauses and swipes at a tear escaping from her eye like she's confused by it. The movement reveals a tattoo that wasn't visible before. Twisting tree branches with beautiful leaves swirl down from her left eye and over her cheek toward her ear. "I know you have questions, and I'm sorry I can't answer them. Rye will answer most of them in a few days." Tawny is staring now at Rye. "Tell her she can come home to us whenever she's ready."

I can't see how Tawny gets the ring onto Rye's swollen hand, but when Tawny shifts position, it's on Rye's finger. I flick my wide eyes to Tawny. She has produced a vial similar to the one in which I saw my first curse. She sets it on the ground beside Rye and pulls up Rye's shirt, exposing the side of her bloated stomach. Chimmi clambers down Tawny's arm onto Rye. The feeling of shock that hits me is intense as I watch one of the hook-shaped claws on Chimmi's strange feet puncture Rye's flesh. Chimmi climbs up Tawny's arm to her shoulder. Nothing immediate is happening with the hole Chimmi poked.

A strong, sweet smell wafts through the air. Tawny is holding a sprig of tubular yellow, pink, and white flowers near the opening in Rye's body. *Honeysuckle!* Tawny is massaging the air over the flower, and the floral smell disappears. I can see by the weaves that she's focusing the smell on the incision. Within seconds, the tiny body of a curse pushes through the incision, followed by a steady flow of others. Tawny's hand is a blur as she deposits the honeysuckle into the vial. The curses follow the flower without thought. Rye's body deflates at an equal rate: the vial is physically growing!

As the vial grows, a pattern becomes visible on the glass. I blink at the silver tree branches with beautiful green leaves like Tawny's ring and tattoo. The leaves on the tree move like they are fluttering in the breeze. As they flutter, the silver branches sparkle and the leaves shimmer. The glass behind them darkens like an angry storm cloud. The stream of curses coming out of Rye's body has withered to a trickle. Then one sole curse comes out. Its flight toward the vial is lethargic and clumsy. As it breaches the rim of the vial, Tawny corks it. The branches and leaves are in a gale-force wind, and the dark mass behind is moving with equal vigour. Then it all stops at once.

I close my eyes to let my brain catch up to the last image. Tawny, the sullen teenager with the pinched facial expression, stands up and stretches. Her body becomes a shimmering mist with a solid mass floating at its centre. The mist falls to the ground like clear glitter leaving a levitating one-inch-tall life form. It spins and flies toward me, stopping just short of my nose. I see a tattooed human face attached to a hairless, naked body. Unlike the curses, this creature has pointy ears, and although its wings are ragged, they are vibrant with colour.

"A faerie," Fin whispers.

I look at the faerie. Her metallic eyes reflect flashes of light that make her whole face glimmer. Her pinched face shifts into a toothy smile. She shifts her gaze toward her own shoulder, and I goggle at the sight of a teeny Chimmi perched there. She zooms toward the vial and encircles it in a blur of colour. The vial shrinks to an impossible size. She scoops it up and flies away, leaving us stunned.

"Is anyone else as gobsmacked as me?" Fin breathes.

Before I can answer, the door that leads up to the dwelling for The Society of the Blood Wind rattles. I jump to my feet, armed with sound vibration orbs. The door doesn't open, but it jerks again. There's a soft tremor under my feet. I move toward the door cautiously. I can't see any wards, so I twist the doorknob. The door convulses like a living muscle. It must be something Kyson did on the other side. A crack runs up from the door frame and across the roof as the banging increases. The ground starts to shake, and the tremors become progressively more violent. The clattering sound is now a loud, echoing groan. Small stones and grit dislodge from the roof and walls.

Fin's voice rises over the noise. "We need to go!" Her hand clamps down on Adria's arm. "Move it, Bwitch." Fin cranks her sideways as she runs. Adria stumbles but is quick to get to her feet. Lord Bradig is almost keeping up with them. He has his axe in his hand, swinging it at Adria's heels, making her run more of a hop-step.

Fin doesn't need to tell us twice. Griffin's hands are making a weave to float Belamey out of the tunnels. I watch for a split second before I race to Rye. I move my hands as Griffin did. Threads of magic weave in and out, making a net that seals itself under Rye's body and lifts her off the floor. As I race after Fin and Lord Bradig into the sparkly tunnel, the net moves with me. Griffin is on my heels with Belamey in tow.

It occurs to me we can't evacuate the way we came in because of the murk monsters. "We don't know how to get out!"

Fin's words are muffled as she stampedes us deeper into the tunnel. "There's a fork up ahead. I'm assuming it leads out since Rye appeared from this tunnel and she wouldn't have got past the murk monsters if she came the way we did."

There's a series of crashes behind us. *Let's hope you're right.* The ruckus echoes deafeningly in the tunnel and all talk ceases as we run for our lives. I see Fin veer to the right. I gear down enough to ensure I don't bounce Rye off the wall when we make the corner. Thankfully, this tunnel sparkles, too. There isn't time to fully appreciate the way the sparkles cast light. I power forward fighting the compulsion to touch them.

Griffin hollers as he rounds the corner. "Tunnel's collapsing!"

The rumbling is so loud that it vibrates my eardrums. The first sparkling tunnel makes sounds like dominoes falling. Fine powder marks the air coating everything with grime. Fin has reached a sketchy-looking wooden ladder. She's climbing for all she's worth, but we won't all get up before this tunnel collapses.

Lord Bradig is hiccupping wildly at the base of the ladder. His glowing eyes are locked on Adria. He's holding his axe, tapping the handle against his other hand while Adria is casting suspicious glances between him and Fin. I'm puzzling ways to get Adria up the ladder because there's no way we can remove her cuffs. Griffin comes to a stop beside me.

"I don't trust the ladder to hold more than one person at a time," I say quietly, looking over the surrounding walls. No cracks yet, but I don't know if that means anything. "How are we going to get her up?"

The smell in the air changes. A draft swirls the familiar aroma of rain and wet earth. I don't need to look to know that Lord Bradig is using his winds. The air currents are visible. They're the same dark blue, with greys and blacks, that he used to clear the tunnel of curses. The currents are swirling faster, their intensity growing. Sparks of electricity flash in the air. I'm having difficulty staying in control of the net floating Rye. I look up to see where Fin is, but I can't see her. I hope she's safe. My eyes pop when I realize Lord Bradig is forming a cone of wind around us, angry funnel cloud winds.

I form a bubble encasing Griffin, Belamey, Rye, Adria, and me. "Lord Bradig, can I extend this sphere to you?" I screech into the wind. A nod is all the concentration that he can spare me. It's enough, I push the bubble out to include him.

Before the swirling wind obscures my view, I see a cloud of dust moving toward us. *The tunnel is failing.* We've lifted off the ground in the vortex of twisting winds.

The roar from the tunnel coming down swirls on the violent air currents. The force of the crumbling shoots a blast of air out under our twister, and we rise with it. My nails are digging into the flesh between my wrist and fingers as I duck my head, waiting for the ceiling to rush up against us. But like an unexpected magic trick, it doesn't. The gale weakens, and I see a starry sky. Then the wind stops, and the bubble drops into the snow, popping. I'm deposited on my butt on the frozen ground. A rush of cold blows over me.

"Did you crack it?" Fin yells. She's muscling a cover over the well we just blew out of. I blink at her, not sure what she's talking about. She straightens, rubs her hands together to brush debris from them, and looks at me. "Did it crack when you landed on it? Your ass, did you crack it?"

I gather a handful of snow and throw it at her. "Where are we?"

She shrugs. "Don't know, Rye entered after us at a different spot. Regardless, we need to go." She flicks her head in the opposite direction. "This is where she entered." I follow her gaze and see the Willys.

We pile in after securing the two magic nets to the vehicle. "Not the safest," I say, staring at Rye and Belamey suspended behind the vehicle.

Fin is eyeing them, too. "Can any of you make magic crash helmets?" She looks up when she's met by our silence, and she shrugs. "I'll drive slow-ish," she says as she steps on the gas.

Chapter 21

Fin knows where we are once we hit the main road. Talon is waiting for us when we return. He hops off the porch, moving his head with jerky movements as he assesses us. Clucking, he ushers us inside. Griffin floats Rye in and heads for the bedroom on the main floor. I float Belamey down to the basement. Nothing is different in the large room that serves as a bedroom, from the unfinished cement floor to the sparse antique pieces of furniture. I pick the first of the four single beds and nestle Belamey under a mound of knitted blankets before returning to the kitchen.

Fin has a hot cup of coffee waiting for me. I smile at her before I delight in a gulp of the steaming brown liquid. Ecstasy, all my tension drains as it slides over my taste buds. If it wasn't so hot, I'd down the full mug. I sigh and slide into a seat at the table. They have placed Adria in the chair in the corner and she looks resigned to her fate, but I'm not fooled. The wheels are spinning behind those sinful blue eyes, trying to plan a way to free herself.

Lord Bradig is standing in front of her, clearly not duped either. He has switched from his axe to his sword and he's tossing it between his hands. A dull clap highlights each pass.

"Is there no grass tea to calm him down?" I whisper to Fin.

She beams a smile at me. "Feisty little guy, isn't he?"

I cock my head and consider him. Feisty isn't the word I would use. The sword is passing hand to hand, resolute and methodical. It's the threatening gesture of a creature who would happily inflict pain, a controlled and disciplined torture. I push aside thoughts of the tongue box. "Is he watching her like that to keep her from running away?" I ask before taking another sip of coffee.

"She can't run," Griffin says from the doorway. I wrinkle my nose questioningly.

"Coffee?" Fin asks.

Griffin shakes his head. He gives Fin a look that makes me blush as he moves toward her. I look away, feeling like I'm intruding on an intimate moment. His voice is low, and I can't hear what he says to her. Fin's grunt of displeasure is a cue that whatever he said wasn't what she wanted to hear. I look over at them. Griffin's lips are separating from Fin's. She gives a soft moan and droops in her chair. My eyes are flicking between them. It's Griffin who speaks. "Adria's cuffs connect to this little device here." He lifts his shirt a bit, exposing a fancy-looking belt buckle. It's coated with dancing threads of magic. "So, she can try to run, but she won't get far and depending on how fast she's moving, she could dislocate her shoulders or rip her arms off completely."

I watch his face, trying to determine if he's joking.

Fin is smiling again. "Imagine if you had handcuffs like that when you were on the police force?"

I blink at her, close my eyes, and shake my head. "Completely inappropriate."

"What? Why? I remember the story you told about . . . shit, what was his name? We went to school with him. Even then, he had a flair for trouble. You know who I mean—the weaselly little guy who likes fire and insults. He was climbing through the protective shield between the front and back seats of your partner's police vehicle while you and Constable . . ." Fin pauses with a surprised look on her face. "What's the matter with me?" Her eyes flash wide. "Is this old age? I can't remember names. I can't . . ."

"Fin!"

"Right. I'm just tired." She sighs and continues. "You and your partner were in an all-out battle with two other guys that had been trying to . . ."

"FIN!"

"What? All I'm saying is, he wouldn't have got

across the street if . . ."

"Blazing hell, give it up."

"Oh, fine," she says. "Inappropriate." She mocks my eye rolls and mumbles, "Not."

"I heard that."

She sticks out her tongue. "You were supposed to."

With a huff, I dramatically swing my eyes to focus on Griffin. "So, now what?"

"Now, I take Adria to Allurist Detention Centre—"

"This place sounds so cool, Kori," Fin interrupts. "It's totally something you would see in the movies. The building itself has its own wards to ensure the safety of the people inside and the public, but each," she pauses, considering her words. She shrugs. "Each jail cell controls the magical strengths of the prisoner placed inside." Her voice increases an octave with each word. "Shit on a stick! That's it, isn't it? Every movie or story comes from some shred of truth." She smacks her hand on the table like she just solved the world's biggest mystery.

There is a touch of sarcasm in my voice. "Sure, Fin." I know enough about regular prisons, so a magical one isn't even a blip on my *I-care* radar. "Griffin, will we see you after you escort Adria to her new home?" I know I shouldn't, but I can't help smiling at Adria.

"You bet we will," Fin says. "He's moving in with us until Cian sends us, The Influencers, on our next mission. I told him you wouldn't mind because you don't. I mean, now that you are getting married, you'll be busy with the wedding preparations."

My eyes almost drop into my coffee cup that froze mid-air. "I am not getting married!"

Griffin gives one of his chuckles, kisses Fin, and motions to Adria to get on her feet. Lord Bradig jumps, aiming his sword up at Adria. "You best behave, you wee sleeven, or I will hunt you down."

Adria slits her eyes at him, ignores the rest of us, and marches into the sunroom. Griffin gives us each a look with his almost clear-coloured eyes and heads after her. As I look after them, I scrunch my face up. "I imagine I'll regret asking this, but how will he escort her there? I thought he said Allurist Detention Centre was a fly-in spot."

Fin passes Bradig a sizeable coffee pot full of grass tea.

Talon looks at me surprised, but then Talon always looks like he's suffering from mild astonishment. "They'll shift into their bird forms. Adria's cuffs will stay bound to her bird legs, and everything will work the same as if they're in human form."

I'm flabbergasted. "But how can she shift? The cuffs control her magic."

"Griffin can manipulate the handcuff's controls to allow that one action, shifting into bird form, to occur."

Satisfied, I heft my coffee cup to my mouth. The silence and the darkness are one outside the window. I watch Fin's face transform into a yawn, and my tiredness is suddenly heavy in my body.

Talon's round eyes are watchful. "You should all get some sleep; it's been a long week. I can watch over Rye and check on Belamey as well."

"A week!"

Talon's head bobs, his Adam's apple moving like a scared worm in his neck. "A week, yes, seven days." He consults his watch. "Yes, yes. It's after midnight."

"It's only been seven days?" I mumble to myself, trying to fit the jumble of activity to the level of soreness and tiredness in my body. Fin pops up and pats Talon on the shoulder as she yawns again.

She spins on me and waits till the yawn fades. "The sperm didn't take. I thought you'd want to know. She tried but wasn't successful." Another yawn overtakes her, and she flows out of the room, leaving me goggling after her.

"I am knackered," Lord Bradig says, following Fin.

Talon rests his eyes on me. "You too, Kori, off you go." He sounds so much like his mother.

I'm overcome with an urge to hug him, and I don't fight it. "Thank you, Talon." I can't imagine him being capable of appearing more surprised, but when I release my embrace, his expression has shot past comical to pure farcical. I cover my giggle with a yawn and head down to the multi-bed bedroom with thoughts of how the cold basement and a bed piled high with heavy blankets are a recipe for a good sleep.

It's morning when I wake. Belamey is still sleeping. I move to his bed to check on him. His intensity is present in his features while he rests. *Priority.* Trembling, I bend to kiss his forehead. Instead, I stifle a sigh when I see that someone has put a candy ring on his ring finger. It reaches the first knuckle. *Fin!* Satisfied that he's resting comfortably, I make my way to the kitchen in search of my favourite hot, bitter drink. I can smell fresh coffee before I get up the stairs. There are voices talking in hushed tones. Fin and Rye sit at the table with a full pot of coffee and clean mugs on a tray between them.

"Morning, Kori." Rye smiles and reaches her arms toward me for a hug.

"Morning," I say, hugging her. "I'm amazed you're awake, Rye. How are you feeling?" I smile a greeting at Fin.

Fin pauses mid-reach for the coffee pot. "Tawny's ring, Kori. It's a faerie ring." She whistles. "Some kind of powerful! Explains how the ring knew things. Remember Tawny saying it knew things? It's a pity it didn't know everything. Anyway, Rye knew about the ring, but I reviewed the don't ever take it off rule with her."

I nod, not 100-percent focused on Fin's words as I

eye the coffee. Fin resumes her reach. As she fills the mugs, I peek into the sunroom. Talon and Lord Bradig are busy with the birds. Fin clears her throat. "Belamey still sleeping?"

I nod and blow on my coffee.

Fin's hands are resting on the table beside her mug. She twists her hand, examining it. "Well, without the faerie ring, he won't heal as quickly. Right, Rye?" She looks at Rye expectantly.

Rye pats Fin's arm. "Yes, Fin."

Fin beams. "Kori, we were waiting for you to wake up to talk about Tawny, Chimmi, and the curses." She rubs her palms together, picks up her coffee, and tips her chair to balance on its hind legs.

Rye laughs. "Okay, Fin. I'll get right into answering what you want to know." She sips her coffee. "As I'm sure you both figured out, Tawny was living among us as a human. It was a disguise that she assumed."

Fin's first interruption happens right away. "Yes, but why did Lord Bradig refer to her as Princess of the Green Fields?"

Good-spirited, Rye laughs again. "Fin, I'll answer everything, but please give me a chance." She smiles. Fin gives her a sheepish grin in return, producing another laugh from Rye. "Tawny's mother is the queen of the faeries, which makes Tawny a princess. Green Fields means the forest."

"Forest faeries," Fin whispers. "So cool!"

"Tawny has been living among us for years, trying to find the bulk of the curses to capture and take home to her mother. I should point out that Tawny and I became friends long before they brought her to live with The Society of the Blood Wind, but she wore a different disguise when we first met."

Fin taps her pointer finger against her nose. "Right, 'cause they thought you to be dead before Tawny was even born. So, you would have had to meet some other time."

Rye is signalling her consensus. "Yes. She took the Tawny persona as a recommendation from me. I knew being a street child would get her inside The Society of the Blood Wind, a pawn for them to manipulate. As you already know, I knew about the curses trapped in the tunnel with Mallory. Tawny was playing a long game, so this cover worked perfectly. She had to ensure she captured all the curses in the tunnels at the same time, because once her cover got blown, she wouldn't be able to return. Living there gave her easy access to the tunnels and information that we wouldn't otherwise have had." Rye pauses to sip her coffee. "Life happens, and she wasn't able to find the curses as quickly as we hoped. Plus, she had to earn trust before she was able to move through the house and outside it without restrictions. Once she was able to start moving freely, we needed to explore the lesser-known and unmapped areas of the tunnels. My movement to and from that area of the tunnels where Mallory was killed is fragmented. We were starting to think that Dolion and Nekane had moved the curses."

I reach for the coffee. "But why did she want to collect the curses? Why would the queen of the fairies want cur—" I pause as my mind conjures up a representation of a curse and the image of Tawny when she transformed into a faerie. So many similarities. My eyes flare with the implication. "Are they related?"

Rye gives a delighted laugh. "Very astute. Although I don't know if the term 'related' is correct. Curses are born from the faerie queen, and they are born as faeries."

Belamey enters the room, taking up where Rye paused. "Faeries are mischievous and can be dangerous." He continues talking as he walks over to Fin, places the candy ring on the table in front of her, and crushes it. "Curses rebel against the faerie ways, extreme rebellion. Some faeries, once tempted by darker habits and tempers, change into—"

"Curses!" Fin says with an explosion of air. Then in a controlled tone. "Fallen faeries, wow!" She sweeps the crushed candy off the table into her hand and pops it into her mouth, winking at Belamey.

"Mother," Belamey says, bending to hug Rye. Her arms latch onto him and hold tight.

I reach for a clean cup and pour Belamey a coffee. I'm assessing him slant-eyed while I pour. He looks healthy and sound. "Does anybody else need a refill?" I ask, sloshing the contents of the pot.

Fin ignores me and tips her head. "Wait, if curses and faeries are birthed in the sense of a mother and her young, then how could the curses breed in Mallory and you?"

"The queen births faeries that can become curses. Faeries themselves have too many other responsibilities to worry about breeding. It's the queen's duty. Curses, though, are different, and they breed only curses."

Fin dismisses the explanation without further thought. "Okay, but how did you already know Tawny?"

Belamey accepts his mug and stays standing behind Rye's chair. Seated where I am beside Rye, the smell of Belamey is strong, cardamom and cedar at the forefront, and it fills me with comfort. Rye gives a sad smile and surprises me by twisting the ring. "That, Fin, is a story for another time."

I notice the ring looks as if it was meant to be worn by her. It fits her middle finger as well as it fits Tawny's finger. Is there significance to the fact that it fits her hand so well? I'm shocked and amused that she's wearing it on her middle finger. Rye sees me staring at her hand and uses it to pat my thigh.

"What will happen to the curses? Will the queen kill them?" I ask quietly.

"No, there will be an attempt to rehabilitate them, I'm unfamiliar with how it'll work for curses born from curses. I imagine, with Chimmi's help, it'll be successful. But if they aren't, then the curses will be contained and cared for until they die of natural causes." She looks at each of us with a smile. "Fin, that leaves your earlier question about Chimmi and Tawny. All I can say is that Chimmi's species comes at a time of great need. Curses, especially in that volume, escaping into the world would be catastrophic. So, I assume that was why he came when he did. Bonding with Tawny is not something I have any knowledge about. But she needed Chimmi's power. The power it took from her to heal Belamey." Rye reaches for him. He places his hand in hers, and she continues. "The power to heal Belamey, remove the curses from me and start my healing, then trap the curses and transport them home," Rye sighs, "should have killed her." She lifts her hand from my leg and brushes the tears on her cheeks. "She would have had to let either Belamey or myself die, possibly both of us."

The silence is heavy. If it wasn't for Lord Bradig's voice booming in the sunroom, we might have remained locked in our silent contemplations. "Cian, the protector, have you come with a new mission for Lord Bradig, the superlative, and," Lord Bradig's voice lowers, but not enough that we can't hear him, "the underlings?"

Cian's husky voice precedes his entrance. "No new mission yet, Lord Bradig? Hello, Talon. How are you?"

I can't hear the first of what Talon says, but I hear him ask, "Will you be staying for lunch?"

"I'm here to collect Rye." Cian steps into the kitchen on thick, powerful legs. His broad shoulders fill the door frame. I'm surprised to see that his face is no longer obscured by grey and black facial hair. He nods to each of us before resting his eyes on Rye.

She blushes under his stare. "Cian."

"Rye."

There's a formality to their greeting that feels falsified.

"So, when is the wedding?" Fin says.

There's a short explosive burst of air and a swirling of black smoke where Belamey was seconds before. I consider initiating my smoky disappearance to avoid explaining to Fin that Belamey hasn't asked me to marry him and I don't know why he would. But when Fin turns her stunned eyes on me, I pause.

"What was that? I meant Cian and Rye?" She flicks her hand dismissively. "You and Belamey need to pop the cherry before marriage becomes a thing."

I blink at her, my irritation warring with my confusion.

"What, you didn't know? Cian and Rye are getting married." Her mouth drops open, and she spins to Rye. "He knows, right? Belamey, I mean, not Cian. He knows you're getting married? That isn't why he did his smoke trick?"

Rye laughs. Fin takes advantage of the time Rye's laughter gives her, and she whispers to me. "The wedding would be a romantic way to lose your divorced woman's virginity. Don't play coy either. I saw how worried you were when he was unconscious. You love him. You're just struggling to admit it. Sealing your feeling with whoopie would be a great way to make Rye's premonition about you two come true."

Rye's laughter has stopped, and I have a moment of panic, thinking she heard the suggestions Fin was making about me and Belamey. But if she heard, she makes no sign.

"He knows, Fin. And he approves. I imagine he's going to get the Bronco from Meeks." Rye stands and moves in to snuggle at Cian's side.

I nearly fall over. His serious chiselled expression transforms into a smile. "Kori, I need you to act in my place for a few days while I'm," he delays allowing his lips to turn up in an unrestrained manner, "otherwise indisposed." He doesn't wait for an answer. He shifts into a sharp-shinned hawk and flies from the room.

"It's grand, Cian, the protector. I am right behind you," Lord Bradig calls as he disappears from sight.

Rye hugs us. "No goodbye, ladies. We shall see each other in one form or another soon." There's a light pop, and we're left looking at sparkling midnight blue smoke in the space that Rye previously occupied.

Fin and I are wearing similar expressions of shock, eyes wide and mouths gaped open.

"Did I hear you mention something about lunch, Talon?" Fin says, quickly adjusting to everyone's abrupt departure. "Let's get cooking . . ."

Chapter 22

Soft snow is falling outside. Inside, it's full of winter's smell. It's a heated, sweet, and spicy fragrance that oozes from the apple cake in the oven. I daydream of a warm slice topped with chopped walnuts and melting vanilla ice cream.

Fin makes an impressive spread of food with things she finds in Talon's fridge and pantry. Four kinds of wraps are cut into petite pieces and laid out on a tray. She's smiling with pride at the feast she created as she introduces the dishes. "These are cranberry salsa turkey wraps, southwest cream cheese chicken wraps, cucumber ranch turkey wraps, and roast beef wraps with dill slaw." She flourishes her hand over the table. "Then we have chickpea salad with lemon and dill, as well as a mandarin mixed green salad."

"Are you expecting company for lunch, Fin?" I ask.

Fin laughs. "Talon is hungry. Right, Talon?"

Astonished, Talon considers the items. "I'm actually quite hungry, now that you mention it."

I bring the coffee pot to the table, and Fin brings a large pitcher of ice water. As she sets the pitcher down, I get a clear view of her shirt, and I choke on my coffee. The smile that cracks across her face is maddening. "I ordered it a couple of days ago and had it delivered here," she says, staring down at the front of herself. There's a unicorn farting out the words "Fin's motto." And underneath in shimmering letters are the words "dark stallions, sparkling unicorns, and insatiable appetites."

"I decided the motto was perfect the way it was. I could have got the print of a unicorn and stallion mating, but that's distasteful." She beams at me.

I blow out a sigh and respond to her with an eye roll. I'm eager to taste the cranberry salsa turkey wrap, and I don't want to get pulled into a back-and-forth conversation about clothing, mottoes, or inappropriate images. Before I put anything else on my plate, I devour my wrap. The tartness of the cranberries is offset by the other ingredients in the salsa, as well as the velvetiness of the cream cheese. Fin sparks up a conversation with Talon about safeguarding. I'm content to let them chat. In the comfort of the moment, I can feel myself relaxing.

"The Influencers is a worthy name," Talon says.

"I ordered matching shirts for the team."

"So, Fin," I say, hiding the smirk that steals across

my face. "You didn't speak to Cian about this name business—"

Her voice jumps over mine. "Didn't seem like an appropriate time." Her eyes squint at me the tiniest bit.

"Scared?"

"I am not! I—"

Loud and impassioned, the bird's elaborate greeting stops my teasing. We all look toward the sunroom as Belamey breaches the doorway. His normal intensity is electric. I take a second to enjoy his toned, athletic build and wait for him to prowl across the room, but he stops. His brown eyes sweep over us.

Something is off. "What is it?" I ask.

Fin perks up beside me. "Belamey? Answer quicker."

He prowls across the kitchen, cups my face with his hands, and presses his lips to mine. I don't fight it. I kiss him back. With a lopsided grin, he scoops up a roast beef dill slaw wrap. As he studies the ingredients, his husky voice comes out low. "I had to stop at Just Flavours after I picked up the Bronco." He takes a big bite and nods his appreciation of the flavours. I roll my eyes.

"You stopped at Just Flavours, and what?"

He sinks his teeth into the wrap eyeing me. He polishes it off before he says anything else. "Found this waiting for us." He lays a piece of brown paper on the table. Someone sealed it shut with a pat of red wax. In the middle of the wax are two sideways flame hands holding swirls.

"That can't be good," Fin says.

"That's what I think. As far as I can tell, there isn't any harmful magic associated with it. Talon? Kori?"

"I don't see any," I pause, considering, "dark magic."

Talon hops closer to the paper. He jerks his head, looking at it from various angles as he pokes it with his pointer finger before he stands up. He shrugs.

Fin crosses her arms and slants her chair. "Well, I'm not opening it!"

"I'll open it." Belamey scoops it off the table with a butter knife. He breaks the seal and opens it before any of us can change our minds.

There are sounds of the flickering crackle of a fire. Then the grating sound of Kyson's voice overwhelms the space. "Our time will come and with it, each of your deaths." There's a brief pause where the only sound is his breathing over the fire, then his voice speaks, listing our names. He drags each one out like he's testing it, savouring it with his personal outline of what's coming. The noise we hear next is strange.

"What are we hearing?" I ask.

"Casket lift," Talon says. His eyes are closed, and he tips his head to the side. "Flame igniting. It must be a lacquered casket."

"Talon?" Fin says with her face screwed into a look of surprise.

Talon's big round eyes fly open. "I worked at a

crematorium."

Kyson is speaking again. His voice is low, "I swear to you, it will be done."

It's strange to see a grimace on Fin's features. "Um, I don't think he's talking to us anymore," she says. The message paper hisses, catches fire, and is a pile of ash in seconds. Fin blows out a sigh. "Well, it's a relief that we won't have to listen to that again because it was off-the-chart shit-ass creepy."

Coming in late 2023/early 2024, a story set approximately forty years before *The Ember Stone.*

An Ember File Side Story

A scream tears through the house with a force that rattles the windows. Ensley's eyes spring wide and she hits the stairs with Aaron on her heels. Their little Juniper Berry is the only other Spellbinder in the house, but for her to give such a piercing cry suggests she may no longer be alone. Neither Ensley nor Aaron gives any conscious thought to the orbs that form in their hands as they pound up the stairs toward their daughter. The silence that follows Juniper Berry's scream is heavy and foreboding . . .

Acknowledgements

Writing a book isn't a single-handed endeavour. With that in mind, I would like to give thanks to the people who helped me bring this book to life.

I can't express enough thanks to my husband and sons for tolerating conversations dominated by my obsession to write and putting up with my daydreaming when I should've been focusing. I loved your suggestions for naming the magical jail in *Chimera and Curses*, and I appreciate every word suggestion you provided when I was struggling for the perfect one to make a sentence shine. Thank you for your love, encouragement, support, and patience.

Big thanks to Laura and Jamie at FriesenPress for helping me make *Chimera and Curses* into the best book it could be.

Thanks to my best friend, Marcia, for being my unofficial title consultant. For me, the title struggle is real and you always make it seem so easy. I remember the title you first helped me tweak in my early blogging years. It remains one of my favourites, *If my children are chipmunks, then toys are nuts!*

Thank you to the Women in Publishing Summit for all the information, sources, and support. It's such an amazing space for a writer to learn in. And thank you to Antoinette, from my blogging world, for introducing me to the Women in Publishing Summit in the first place.

Thank you to my, blog followers. Your support and positive comments encouraged me to challenge myself with longer writing projects. You introduced me to a world of writers that I didn't know existed. Write on my friends!

To my readers, thank you for coming along on this journey with me. Your support inspires me to write each story till its end. I hope that you enjoyed Kori and her team's adventures and I hope you will enjoy whatever the future has in store for these characters.

Without all of you, *Chimera and Curses* would be an incomplete, unshared story hiding on the bookshelf in my mind.

Book Club Reading Guide

1. What was your expectation about the book before you read it?
2. How did this book compare to similar books you've read by other authors?
3. If a movie was being made from this book, who would you cast for the characters?
4. Was this book more of a page-turner or something you needed to take your time reading?
5. Is this book's genre the type you would usually read? If you usually read this genre, why do you prefer it?
6. Did you like or dislike this author's writing style?
7. Do you like the point-of-view the author used? Do you prefer books written from a certain point of view?
8. Did any of the characters feel like someone you know in real life?
9. If you were a character in this book, who would you be?
10. If you could change something that happened in the story, what would you change?

www.ingramcontent.com/pod-product-compliance
Lightning Source LLC
Chambersburg PA
CBHW061154210726
48294CB00006B/1671